DATE DUE

GAYLORD		PRINTED IN U.S.A.

Christopher Paolini

WHO WROTE THAT?

LOUISA MAY ALCOTT
JANE AUSTEN
AVI
L. FRANK BAUM
JUDY BLUME, SECOND EDITION
BETSY BYARS
MEG CABOT
BEVERLY CLEARY
ROBERT CORMIER
BRUCE COVILLE
ROALD DAHL
CHARLES DICKENS
ERNEST J. GAINES
THEODOR GEISEL
S.E. HINTON
WILL HOBBS
ANTHONY HOROWITZ
STEPHEN KING
URSULA K. LE GUIN
MADELEINE L'ENGLE
GAIL CARSON LEVINE
C.S. LEWIS, SECOND EDITION
LOIS LOWRY
ANN M. MARTIN
STEPHENIE MEYER
L.M. MONTGOMERY
PAT MORA
WALTER DEAN MYERS
ANDRE NORTON
SCOTT O'DELL
CHRISTOPHER PAOLINI
BARBARA PARK
KATHERINE PATERSON
GARY PAULSEN
RICHARD PECK
TAMORA PIERCE
DAVID "DAV" PILKEY
EDGAR ALLAN POE
BEATRIX POTTER
PHILIP PULLMAN
MYTHMAKER: THE STORY OF J.K. ROWLING, SECOND EDITION
MAURICE SENDAK
SHEL SILVERSTEIN
LEMONY SNICKET
GARY SOTO
JERRY SPINELLI
R.L. STINE
EDWARD L. STRATEMEYER
MARK TWAIN
E.B. WHITE
LAURA INGALLS WILDER
LAURENCE YEP
JANE YOLEN

Christopher Paolini

John Bankston

Foreword by
Kyle Zimmer

Christopher Paolini

Chelsea House
An imprint of Infobase Publishing
132 West 31st Street
New York, NY 10001

Library of Congress Cataloging-in-Publication Data
Bankston, John, 1974–
Christopher Paolini / John Bankston.
p. cm. — (Who wrote that?)
Includes bibliographical references and index.
ISBN 978-1-60413-727-9 (hardcover)
1. Paolini, Christopher—Juvenile literature. 2. Fantasy fiction—Authorship—Juvenile literature. 3. Authors, American—21st century—Biography—Juvenile literature. 4. Children's stories—Authorship—Juvenile literature. I. Title. II. Series.
PS3616.A55Z59 2010
813'.6—dc22
[B] 2010001366

Chelsea House books are available at special discounts when purchased in bulk quantities for business, associations, institutions, or sales promotions. Please call our Special Sales Department in New York at (212) 967-8800 or (800) 322-8755.

You can find Chelsea House on the World Wide Web at http://www.chelseahouse.com.

Text design by Keith Trego
Cover design by Alicia Post
Composition by EJB Publishing Services
Cover printed by Bang Printing, Brainerd, MN
Book printed and bound by Bang Printing, Brainerd, MN
Date printed: October 2010
Printed in the United States of America

10 9 8 7 6 5 4 3 2 1

This book is printed on acid-free paper.

All links and Web addresses were checked and verified to be correct at the time of publication. Because of the dynamic nature of the Web, some addresses and links may have changed since publication and may no longer be valid.

Table of Contents

FOREWORD BY
KYLE ZIMMER
PRESIDENT, FIRST BOOK

HUMANITY IS POWERED by stories. From our earliest days as thinking beings, we employed every available tool to tell each other stories. We danced, drew pictures on the walls of our caves, spoke, and sang. All of this extraordinary effort was designed to entertain, recount the news of the day, explain natural occurrences—and then gradually to build religious and cultural traditions and establish the common bonds and continuity that eventually formed civilizations. Stories are the most powerful force in the universe; they are the primary element that has distinguished our evolutionary path.

Our love of the story has not diminished with time. Enormous segments of societies are devoted to the art of storytelling. Book sales in the United States alone topped $24 billion in 2006; movie studios spend fortunes to create and promote stories; and the news industry is more pervasive in its presence than ever before.

There is no mystery to our fascination. Great stories are magic. They can introduce us to new cultures, or remind us of the nobility and failures of our own, inspire us to greatness or scare us to death; but above all, stories provide human insight on a level that is unavailable through any other source. In fact, stories connect each of us to the rest of humanity not just in our own time, but also throughout history.

This special magic of books is the greatest treasure that we can hand down from generation to generation. In fact, that spark in a child that comes from books became the motivation for the creation of my organization, First Book, a national literacy program with a simple mission: to provide new books to the most disadvantaged children. At present, First Book has been at work in hundreds of communities for over a decade. Every year children in need receive millions of books through our organization and millions more are provided through dedicated literacy institutions across the United States and around the world. In addition, groups of people dedicate themselves tirelessly to working with children to share reading and stories in every imaginable setting from schools to the streets. Of course, this Herculean effort serves many important goals. Literacy translates to productivity and employability in life and many other valid and even essential elements. But at the heart of this movement are people who love stories, love to read, and want desperately to ensure that no one misses the wonderful possibilities that reading provides.

When thinking about the importance of books, there is an overwhelming urge to cite the literary devotion of great minds. Some have written of the magnitude of the importance of literature. Amy Lowell, an American poet, captured the concept when she said, "Books are more than books. They are the life, the very heart and core of ages past, the reason why men lived and worked and died, the essence and quintessence of their lives." Others have spoken of their personal obsession with books, as in Thomas Jefferson's simple statement: "I live for books." But more compelling, perhaps, is the almost instinctive excitement in children for books and stories.

Throughout my years at First Book, I have heard truly extraordinary stories about the power of books in the lives of children. In one case, a homeless child, who had been bounced from one location to another, later resurfaced—and the only possession that he had fought to keep was the book he was given as part of a First Book distribution months earlier. More recently, I met a child who, upon receiving the book he wanted, flashed a big smile and said, "This is my big chance!" These snapshots reveal the true power of books and stories to give hope and change lives.

As these children grow up and continue to develop their love of reading, they will owe a profound debt to those volunteers who reached out to them—a debt that they may repay by reaching out to spark the next generation of readers. But there is a greater debt owed by all of us—a debt to the storytellers, the authors, who have bound us together, inspired our leaders, fueled our civilizations, and helped us put our children to sleep with their heads full of images and ideas.

WHO WROTE THAT? is a series of books dedicated to introducing us to a few of these incredible individuals. While we have almost always honored stories, we have not uniformly honored storytellers. In fact, some of the most important authors have toiled in complete obscurity throughout their lives or have been openly persecuted for the uncomfortable truths that they have laid before us. When confronted with the magnitude of their written work or perhaps the daily grind of our own, we can forget that writers are people. They struggle through the same daily indignities and dental appointments, and they experience the intense joy and bottomless despair that many of us do. Yet somehow they rise above it all to deliver a powerful thread that connects us all. It is a rare honor to have the opportunity that these books provide to share the lives of these extraordinary people. Enjoy.

Bestselling novelist Carl Hiaasen is seen attending the Los Angeles premiere of Hoot*, a 2006 film based on his critically acclaimed young-adult novel of the same name. On a trip with his family, Hiaasen discovered Christopher Paolini's self-published first novel,* Eragon*, in a Montana grocery store.*

1

Lucky Break

CARL HIAASEN STARED at the row of books in a Montana grocery store. The titles lining the shelves were familiar—the same ones he would have encountered in New York City or his home in Florida.

The books stocked by the supermarket chain were mostly popular fiction—those among the thousands of books published annually that appear on best-seller lists published in periodicals like the *New York Times*. Hiaasen was quite familiar with such books that sell millions of copies and earn their authors millions of dollars. It was what he did for a living.

A reporter at the *Miami Herald*, Hiaasen wrote his first few novels as collaborations with another author, until he struck out on his own in 1983 with *Tourist Season*. That novel, and most of the ones that followed, combined mystery and dark humor with Hiaasen's abiding love for the environment and his concerns about unchecked development in Florida. In a review for *Chicago Tribune Books*, Gary Dretzka explained that Hiaasen "displays no mercy for anyone perceived as being responsible for defiling his home environment."[1]

Hiaasen's first novel for younger readers, 2002's *Hoot*, won a prestigious Newbery Honor Award from the American Library Association. Hiaasen later explained his motivation for shifting away from writing strictly for adult audiences. "My stepson, nephews and nieces are always bugging me about reading one of my books. . . . I created the same sensibilities in my kid characters that my adult ones walk around with."[2]

In fact, his 11-year-old stepson, Ryan, was the reason why Hiaasen and his wife were seeking a book in a grocery store. It was a long drive to Missoula, Montana. The right book would be a perfect diversion. If only they could find it.

"My wife stumbles on this book called *Eragon*, and we asked somebody and they said, 'Oh, that's local,' because it didn't have an imprint of a publisher," Hiaasen recalled in an interview.

> It was still nice, but it was clearly not a book that came from a New York publishing house. . . . She threw it at Ryan and she said, "You're reading this in the car; this looks good." And so he grumbled and he complained as kids that age will do, and yet we didn't hear from him for hours. . . .

> And I keep looking back and his nose is in the book and I think he finished it the next day. It was unbelievable. And he said, "This is better than *Harry Potter*."[3]

If not for his stepson, Hiaasen might never have purchased the book. If not for his "second career" writing young adult fiction, Hiaasen might not have read it later. He was, however, captured by the fantasy just as his stepson had been. Hiaasen then called his editor in New York. Their conversation was one that aspiring novelists imagine—the life-changing moment that connects them to the lofty world of major publishers and just-as-major book deals. It was a magical bit of fate. Eragon, the 15-year-old hero of the book, would have appreciated it.

A DREAM FULFILLED

For every novel published by a major New York publishing house like Simon & Schuster or Random House, many thousands of manuscripts are rejected. A few spunky authors turn to self-publishing. They quickly realize writing a book and selling a book are two radically different occupations. Exhausting their sales to friends, family, coworkers, and other acquaintances, they rarely sell more than 100 copies. Self-published novels generally do not appear on a supermarket's shelf. Instead, they reside in unopened boxes or stacked in garages, attics, or basements.

By the time Carl Hiaasen read *Eragon*, it had already sold more than 10,000 copies. The number was not achieved by sterling connections, a clever advertising campaign, or a flashy Web site. In fact, the author was just a teenager. After earning his high school diploma through a correspondence program, 15-year-old Christopher Paolini decided against college in order to spend a year writing his novel and another year editing it. The project became a family enterprise. Not only did his parents help him polish his prose, they also published it.

"They literally sold the book out of the trunk of his dad's car," Hiaasen explained.[4] "For a while, money was so tight that if we didn't sell books, we didn't eat," Christopher Paolini's father, Kenneth, conceded to the *Daily Telegraph*.[5]

Once the book was ready to be sold, Paolini embarked on an ingenious marketing campaign. "I wore knee-high black lace-up leather boots, black pantaloons, a big black pirate belt, a billowy red swordsman shirt and a black beret to top it off," he later described to *USA Today*.[6] Thus attired as a Renaissance storyteller, Paolini gave over 150 presentations in libraries and auditoriums. The feat is even more

Did you know...

The Web site SelfPublishingResources.com lists numerous well-known examples of successful books that began as self-published works. Among them, William Strunk Jr.'s *Elements of Style*, which was originally produced just for his Cornell University students; *The Celestine Prophecy* by James Redfield, which has sold over 20 million copies worldwide; and the career counseling handbook *What Color is Your Parachute?* by Richard N. Bolles. Along with *Eragon*, most of the self-published books listed here sold only a few thousand copies before a major publisher signed their authors.

impressive when one considers that the author had never actually attended a school.

Impressed by Paolini's raw talent and verve, Knopf editor Michelle Frey offered the author a contract. "I was in Seattle at the Northwest Bookfest, promoting the original edition of *Eragon*," Paolini remembered. "My first reaction was one of disbelief, since I had no idea how Michelle could have heard about *Eragon*."[7]

Christopher Paolini was then barely 18 years old. An editor thousands of miles away was prepared to change his whole life. Yet Paolini took his time. For like the hero of his first novel, Paolini sought to choose his own destiny. If a publisher wanted his novel, it would be on his own terms. After all, living life on one's own terms was how his parents taught him to live. It was a lesson they learned when they left Southern California for a rough-hewn existence in Montana's Paradise Valley.

The altar of the Church Universal and Triumphant (CUT) chapel in Corwin Springs, Montana, reveals the group's diverse influences, from Buddha, at left, to the Virgin Mary, near the center. A photo of the church's spiritual leader, Elizabeth Clare Prophet, is also on the altar. Christopher Paolini's parents were CUT members for several years.

2

Land of Dragons

KENNETH PAOLINI and Talita Hodgkinson met because of fantastic visitations described by a teenager. Unlike their future son's dragon, the visits Mark Prophet described did not become a book. They became a religion.

Inspired by those visions, Mark Prophet founded the Summit Lighthouse in 1958. Three years later, he met fellow acolyte Elizabeth Claire Wolf at Boston University. She also claimed to have experienced divine visitation. The two married in 1965. Eight years later, after her husband's death, Elizabeth Prophet founded the Church Universal and Triumphant (CUT). Based first in Pasadena, California, and then in

Malibu, California, the church was "dedicated to spreading the teachings of the Ascended Masters," according to the web site allaboutcults.org. "Ascended Masters are persons who once lived on earth. By the experience of Reincarnation, they have, through trial and testing, rid themselves of negative Karma, have become perfected, and have ascended back to their divine source or 'God.' "[1]

Mark Prophet claimed to have seen an Ascended Master named El Morya when he was 17 years old. A different Ascended Master, Saint Germain, supposedly visited his future wife. Mark and Elizabeth Prophet believed that Ascended Masters also included such spiritual leaders as Moses, Jesus, and Buddha.

CUT—with its belief in karma, reincarnation, and other hallmarks of Eastern religions—attracted many followers to California, including Kenneth Paolini and Talita Hodgkinson, who were interested in non-traditional belief systems. However, as a biography of Elizabeth Prophet notes, both she and CUT "endured a steady stream of attacks from former church members and the anti-cult movement. She has been denounced as a charismatic leader who controls the life of church members."[2] Those fears escalated in the fall of 1978.

JONESTOWN

A few hundred miles north of CUT, in San Francisco, another religious cult, the People's Temple, was also being run by a charismatic leader. And just like with CUT, outsiders feared he exercised too much control over his congregation.

An only child, Jim Jones was born in rural Indiana where he endured both poverty and abuse. In 1954, when he was in his early twenties, he founded the People's Temple as the

Reverend James Jones, founder of the People's Temple, clasps an unidentified man at Jonestown on November 18, 1978, during Congressman Leo J. Ryan's visit. Shortly after, Ryan, newsman Don Harris, cameraman Bob Brown, and San Francisco Examiner *photographer Greg Robinson, who took this photo, were killed in Port Kaituma, Guyana.*

state's first biracial church. Its membership was predominantly African American, but its leaders were mainly white like Jones. A Marxist, Jones used his ministry to promote socialism, the political philosophy advocating the abolishment of private property. His sermons often championed the redistribution of wealth from rich to poor—a popular message for his impoverished congregants. He also claimed he was reincarnated from Jesus, Buddha, and Vladimir Lenin, the famed Bolshevik leader.

After relocating to San Francisco in 1972, Jones was supported by numerous celebrities and liberals who respected his beliefs. More African Americans also joined because of his traditional evangelical preaching style. He was so popular, in fact, that Mayor George Moscone appointed Jones to the San Francisco Housing Authority. By then, however, the People's Temple was attracting more critics than supporters. Some claimed Jones physically punished church members and that the Temple prevented them from speaking to relatives while forcing them to donate most of their income. But by then, Jones was already planning his organization's next move.

In 1974, the People's Temple had leased nearly 4,000 acres in Guyana, in South America. Members cleared the land for farming. They called it Jonestown. "During 1977," according to *World of Criminal Justice*, "amid bad publicity, lawsuits, and relatives' complaints, Jones and nearly 1,000 followers—three-quarters black, two-thirds female, almost one-third under eighteen—moved to Jonestown. Social Security and welfare checks followed."[3] By then the church's assets exceeded $10 million.

Despite the relocation, claims of abuse continued to dog Jones. "Charges that overwork, poor food, harsh punishments, tranquilizers, armed guards, censored mail and phone calls . . . made Jonestown tantamount to a concentration camp led Congressman Leo J. Ryan to visit in late 1978,"[4] the *World of Criminal Justice* continues. Ryan's visit to Jonestown, however, was pleasant and included both music and a barbecue. Afterward, the congressman left with 16 residents who wanted to return to the United States. As they boarded two planes on a nearby runway, men on a flatbed truck and a man in one of the planes began firing rifles. Ryan and four others were killed.

Back in Jonestown, Jones asked his members to commit suicide. Nearly all complied. More than 900 men, women, and children died after drinking cyanide and grape-flavored punch. Jones died from a gunshot, presumably self-inflicted.

In the aftermath, "alternative churches" like CUT were seen as potentially dangerous cults. Like Jones's cult, CUT predicted an eminent apocalypse and earned millions of dollars from members who donated their income and assets. Members were also discouraged from interacting with non–church members, including members of their own families.

Although a reporter in a *New York Times* article once described CUT as a "survivalist group with a doomsday philosophy,"[5] Kenneth Paolini and Talita Hodgkinson appreciated the church's non-traditional beliefs. They believed they could survive without help from outsiders, including government agencies or employers. In the early 1980s, CUT began transforming itself into an exclusive, self-reliant community by purchasing hundreds of acres in Montana. In 1986, the organization would relocate their headquarters to the state.

After getting married, Talita and Kenneth Paolini honeymooned in Maui. Kenneth Paolini told a reporter that while hiking through the Haleakala volcano, they decided that "one of the templates for our relationship would be that our family would come first. All our financial decisions were based on how we can stay together."[6]

The Paolinis proved their self-reliance during Talita Paolini's pregnancy. They did not want to rely on a hospital or a doctor. Instead, she gave birth at home. On November 17, 1983, Christopher Paolini was born in California.

At the time, the couple still belonged to CUT. Christopher's sister, Angela, was also born at home two years later. By then CUT, led by Elizabeth Prophet, believed the world was coming to an end.

DOOMSDAY PROPHET

The 1980s represented a period of growth for CUT, as the Cold War between the United States and the Union of Soviet Socialist Republics (USSR) escalated. Each side increased military spending and built large stockpiles of conventional and nuclear weapons. Many feared it was likely that the two nations could plunge the world into a nuclear war. Against this backdrop, films like *Testament* and the television movie *The Day After*, both released in 1983, portrayed the horrific aftermath of nuclear war between the two superpowers.

Expecting nuclear warheads to level urban areas, Prophet purchased land far from the cities in the Paradise Valley section of Montana. "Church leader Elizabeth Clare Prophet had said nuclear war was likely, and bombs could land in Paradise Valley," explained the *Bozeman Daily Chronicle.* "Church members hoped the bombs would never launch, but they wanted to be prepared if the missiles did fly."[7]

Prophet used her church's wealth to not only purchase hundreds of acres of Montana ranchland, but also to construct what would become the largest privately owned bomb shelter in the United States. Along with a smaller underground shelter in the Paradise Valley subdivision of Glastonbury, the church built one in a mountain meadow of the Royal Teton Ranch capable of protecting more than 700 devotees.

On March 15, 1990, hundreds of believers were instructed to enter the shelters. Some arrived from the far edges of

Christopher Paolini's family settled in Paradise Valley, north of Yellowstone National Park, in Montana, after leaving CUT. Such wide-open vistas would inspire the young author's fantasy epic.

the United States. Others came from South America and Europe. They maxed out credit cards, emptied savings accounts, and quit jobs. The mass arrival attracted the attention of Montana locals and the national media.

CUT members hunkered down in the shelters and waited for a nuclear holocaust. "Then, nothing happened," explained reporter Scott McMillion. "Church officials maintained the next day the whole thing had been a drill. But some members didn't know that: before they left their shelters, they turned on the Geiger counters."[8] The instruments were designed to measure radioactivity; members wanted to see how dangerous the nuclear fallout was before they ventured into the outside world.

Because there was no war, the exercise greatly reduced the number of CUT true believers. The Paolinis, however, had missed the nonevent. According to the *New York Times*, the family had left CUT three years earlier, in 1987. "We weren't willing to surrender our family to the group,"[9] Kenneth Paolini later explained.

DO IT YOURSELF

Following an Alaskan sojourn, the Paolinis settled in Montana in 1991. Despite their disagreements with CUT, they had fallen in love with the state. The family settled in Paradise Valley. North of Yellowstone National Park and in the shadow of the Beartooth Mountains, it attracts both vacationing movie stars and filmmakers. The 1992 movie *A River Runs Through It* was shot a few miles from the Paolinis' simple beige wood-and-shingle home.

Compared to California, Montana's lower tax rates and cost of living made it easier for the couple to be self-sufficient and earn a living without relying on an employer. Kenneth Paolini worked as a photographer and offered a form of deep tissue massage called Rolfing. His wife wrote instructional materials. They also collaborated on a number of books, including *Psychic Dictatorship in America* and *400 Years of Imaginary Friends: A Journey into the World of Adepts, Masters, Ascended Masters, and Their Messengers*, which critically examined one of their former church's core beliefs. They also published educational books, such as *Play and Learn with Cereal O's: Simple, Effective Activities to Help You Educate Your Preschool Child*. These works reflected their passion for educating their children.

Instead of approaching publishers with their work, the couple published the books themselves. They mastered desktop publishing computer programs and earned money selling the works to the public. While their books were not huge sellers, the knowledge they gained from the process served them well.

THE MONTESSORI METHOD

In addition to these ventures, Talita Paolini was also certified in the Montessori teaching method developed by Maria Montessori. Born in Italy in 1870, Montessori was the first woman admitted to the University of Rome's medical school, at a time when she required the support of a pope in order to do so. Following her graduation, her career shifted from a private practice to working with mentally challenged and homeless children.

As she focused on education over medicine, Montessori developed a philosophy that "children best learned such tasks as reading and writing at the age of three or four," according to *Contemporary Authors Online*. She believed a child's intelligence was not fixed and that his or her environment was a major factor in its development. The article goes on to note:

> [C]entral to her theories was the tenet that teachers should stay in the background as much as possible, allowing the child to learn as independently as possible. She also placed great emphasis on the idea that the child's own interest in learning

was sufficiently strong that no rewards or punishments were needed in the educational process.[10]

In fact, her belief in a child's independence was so strong that she did not even believe small children should have a specific bedtime. Left to their own devices, she believed children would sleep when they needed to.

Public schools were reluctant to adopt her techniques, but private schools approved by the Association Montessori Internationale flourished in the United States. Although her core beliefs have often been ignored by traditional schools that are focused more on achievement in standardized tests than in individual development, her influence is felt even there: She was, for example, the first educator to utilize now-standard child-size tables and chairs in her classrooms.

As a Montessori teacher, Talita Paolini wanted to make sure learning was never boring. Christopher, however, resisted his mother's efforts. In a later interview, he described himself:

> "I hate to read!" cried the little boy obstinately. "I don't see why I have to learn this, I'm never going to use it." That's what I said nearly fifteen years ago when Mom was teaching me how to read. Back then I knew that reading wasn't part of my world and I knew that it was just a waste of time. Mom was patient, though, and carefully guided me until I could read simple words. Then she took me to the library.[11]

The event was transformative. "I found in the children's section a series of mystery books with bright covers and splashy spines," he recalled in a 2003 Author Talk.

> I checked one out, and when I read it, it was as if something clicked in my head: all of a sudden I could hear the dialogue, I

could see the characters, and I could smell their surroundings. It was like magic! From that day on, I've been in love with the written word.[12]

The proof of this love lay in the list of books Christopher checked out from his local library—reportedly more than 3,000 different titles before he turned 16. His sister, Angela, checked out about as many during the same time period.

HOMESCHOOLING

Having preschoolers at home led Talita Paolini to make a life-changing decision. Just as the Paolini parents had decided they did not want the Church Universal and Triumphant making decisions about their lives, they realized they did not want outsiders making decisions about their children's education.

Did you know...

Among the more than 3,000 titles Christopher Paolini says he checked out from his local library before he turned 16 are numerous books in the Ramona, Nancy Drew, and Tom Swift series, along with Anne McCaffrey's Dragonriders of Pern series. He also enjoyed novels by J.R.R. Tolkien, Brian Jacques, E.R. Eddison, David Eddings, and Ursula K. Le Guin, as well as Raymond E. Feist's *Magician* and Seamus Heaney's translation of *Beowulf*. As a teen he also read books about writing, including *Characters and Viewpoint* by Orson Scott Card and Robert McKee's *Story*.

In an interview, Christopher Paolini noted that homeschooling was an educational decision:

> By the time we were old enough to be enrolled in first grade we were already several grades ahead of where we would normally be, age wise. Since my parents didn't want to hold us back and also didn't want to stick us in school with children several years older than we were, they decided to homeschool us, which was quite a decision because it meant at any given time one of my parents had to be at home and couldn't be working.[13]

It also meant a more free-flowing education. Most public schools in the United States are required by state and federal regulations to teach certain information, at certain times. Homeschooled children in Montana, however, are not saddled with those requirements. "There are absolutely no testing requirements, standardized or otherwise, for homeschooled children in Montana," notes the Web site eHow.com. "Montana acts on the legal belief that a parent is solely responsible for the education of their child. In the setting of a homeschool, that means that the actual curriculum taught, resources used, assessments used, and method of teaching cannot be dictated by anyone to the parent."[14]

As a Montessori educator, Talita Paolini believed in letting her children's natural curiosity inspire the lessons. While she sought to make sure they learned the basics in math, science, English, and the like, many lessons began with Christopher and Angela. A question about a mountain range could lead not only to a lesson about geography or science, but also about the history of the area, the mathematical formula for determining the mountain's dimensions, or even a civics lessons regarding a local group's efforts to preserve ancient trails.

When Christopher became curious about pirates, he created his own map—soaking it in tea and burning the edges to make it look authentic. Noticing Angela's interest in cats, their mother gave her a book of cat stickers, which inspired Angela to write stories about them. "They taught us how to think," she told a reporter.[15] Moreover, the children were encouraged to conduct research on their own and follow their own bliss. Kenneth Paolini wanted his children to have the time "to watch the clouds, to have thinking space."[16]

Christopher remains grateful for the education his parents gave them. In an interview with BookBrowse, he admitted, "Everything I did was only possible because my parents were dedicated and loving enough to homeschool my sister and me."[17]

While he and many other homeschooled students feel blessed, some educators, especially those who work for public schools, are critical of the practice. "If they were presenting something that met the needs of students both socially and academically, it would be worth looking at, but that's not the case,"[18] offered Richard C. Iannuzzi, president of the New York State United Teachers union, when confronted by the increasing number of parents who opt to homeschool their children.

Even Christopher Paolini admits that his education was not well rounded. Although he read thousands of books far above his grade level, he admitted in his late teens that he knew "nothing about math."[19]

A WRITER IS BORN

Christopher Paolini was enjoying fairly complex novels even as his peers entered elementary school. Around age 12, he developed a fascination with fantasy and science fiction. He read Frank Herbert's *Dune* and Anne McCaffrey's Dragonriders of Pern series, as well as the works of famed sci-fi and fantasy authors like Ursula K. Le Guin.

These works and others inspired him to write science fiction and fantasy stories. So, too, did the place where he grew up. "I've been imagining these things for years, for as long as I can remember," he explained in an interview with the London *Telegraph*. "We live in this beautiful place—they got the name right when they called it Paradise Valley—and my dad always had this great collection of science-fiction books, so it got me started."[20]

The Paolinis did not watch television, but the family enjoyed movies on videotape and later DVD. Christopher feels the power of film pales beside the power of literature. "Books are the greatest device for transporting you into another person's mind," he explained in a 2003 interview. "Movies excel at depicting action with a bit of talk, theater excels at depicting talk with a bit of action, and radio is all talk. But books can take you deeper into people's thoughts and feelings than any other media."[21] He believes, however, that knowing about these forms of expression is fundamentally important for an artist. "If you are going to be creating art," Christopher told *Time for Kids*, "you need to be familiar with different forms of that art."[22]

He did not come up with completely original stories at first. Christopher's teenage efforts were similar to those of another famous writer, Stephen King, who noted in his book *On Writing*:

> You may find yourself adopting a style you find particularly exciting, and there's nothing wrong with that. When I read Ray Bradbury as a kid, I wrote like Ray Bradbury—everything green and wondrous and seen through a lens smeared with the grease of nostalgia. When I read James M. Cain, everything

> I wrote came out clipped and stripped and hard-boiled. When I read Lovecraft, my prose became luxurious and Byzantine. I wrote stories in my teenage years where all these styles merged, creating a kind of hilarious stew. This sort of stylistic blending is a necessary part of developing one's own style, but it doesn't occur in a vacuum. You have to read widely.[23]

TOLKIEN AND HEANEY

In later interviews, Paolini explained he wanted his writing to be as good as the best work by J.R.R. Tolkien and Seamus Heaney's translation of *Beowulf*. "The poem called *Beowulf* was composed sometime between the middle of the seventh and the end of the tenth century of the first millennium, in the language that is today called Anglo Saxon or Old English," Heaney explained in the introduction to his translation.

> It is a heroic narrative, more than three thousand lines long, concerning the deeds of a Scandinavian prince, also called Beowulf, and it stands as one of the foundation works of poetry in English. . . . [*Beowulf*] is a work of the greatest imaginative vitality, a masterpiece where the structuring of the tale is as elaborate as the beautiful contrivances of its language.[24]

It comes as no surprise that Paolini admired both Heaney's translation and Tolkien's writing, as Tolkien admired the epic poem so much as a professor at Oxford University in England that he authored a now-famous paper on it: "*Beowulf*: The Monsters and the Critics." Shortly after the paper was published, Tolkien's first major novel, *The Hobbit*, was published in 1937. Its epic quality was likely inspired in part by *Beowulf*. Yet *The Hobbit* was but the beginning of Tolkien's work.

Published in three volumes in 1954 and 1955, nearly two decades after *The Hobbit*, the sprawling epic *The Lord of the Rings* gave Tolkien both wealth and fame. It also provided a template for aspiring fantasy writers everywhere. A story based on legends but existing in a world entirely of the author's creation, the novel depicted the classic hero's journey. Frodo Baggins, nephew of *The Hobbit*'s hero, Bilbo, was the tale's unlikely hero. Because of their heroes' connection, critics have often compared the two works.

"*The Hobbit* continues to be a story written for extremely intelligent children of all ages and [the novel's protagonist] Bilbo Baggins seems to me easier to accept and like than his heroic nephew Frodo Baggins, the protagonist of the long and complicated *The Lord of the Rings*," Harold Bloom wrote in his introduction to *Modern Critical Views: J.R.R. Tolkien*. "I think we are fond of [Bilbo Baggins] because he is a hobbit to whom things happen . . . [his] preferences for comfort and a sleepy existence persuade because of their universality."[25]

"Tolkien can employ many of the traditional figures of fairy tales like wizards, dwarves, and elves and can work to make them as impressive and as powerful as he likes," explained Roger Sale in his essay "Tolkien and Frodo Baggins," "but that they must always be a little irrelevant because Frodo, neither impressive nor powerful, is Ring-bearer at the moment, and is at least as able to accomplish its destruction as anyone else, even though he has no credentials as a hero whatsoever."[26]

Inspired by such epic works, Christopher Paolini began imagining his own unlikely hero, a boy with the same weaknesses as his own. Unfortunately his early writing was not just imitative. It was also unfinished. "When I was 13 and 14, I made several stabs at writing down some of the epics I constantly daydreamed about," he later explained. "However, they always petered out after five or ten pages, mainly because I didn't know what should happen next with the characters. I realized that I needed to learn how to construct strong plots that could be sustained over the course of an entire novel."[27]

Despite the influences of more complex works of literature, a creature from a simpler book ultimately inspired Christopher's epic. At 12, he had enjoyed reading *Jeremy Thatcher, Dragon Hatcher*, a novel by Bruce Coville. In a 2003 Author Talk, he explained: "I see gigantic, majestic flying dragons. I have visions of them all the time, whether I'm in the shower, sitting on the couch, or riding in the car. The problem with dragons is that they tend to take over your mind. That is why I was compelled to write my novel."[28]

The work would take more than two years to complete. It would also change the life not only of Christopher Paolini, but the lives of his entire family as well.

The Ring cycle of operas written by famed German composer Richard Wagner (1813–1883) helped to inspire much of Christopher Paolini's writing, forming a "soundtrack" to his Inheritance fantasy series.

3

Writing *Eragon*

BECAUSE HE AND his sister were homeschooled, Christopher Paolini was not a typical high school student. He did not go to proms or pep rallies; there were no homecoming dances or large graduation ceremonies. Not attending high school also meant he skipped put-downs and peer pressure, fights in the hallway, and bullies on the playground. He was never told that his love for reading was "weird," his interest in dragons "geeky," or his appreciation of classical music "lame." All in all, he has no regrets.

"You can't miss what you've never had or experienced, really," he told the *Courier-Mail.* "I had friends growing up, there were other homeschoolers we were in touch with, so we weren't isolated and I've always been happily engaged in my own projects and pursuing my own goals."[1]

Although Paolini was not completely removed from his peer group, he was sheltered from knowing teenagers with more typical high school experiences. Had he interacted with more of them, he might have discovered their primary goal. Most teenagers want to be adults. And many adults do not read—or discuss their interest in—science fiction and fantasy writing.

Ursula K. Le Guin has been working in these genres for decades. In her essay, "Why Americans are Afraid of Dragons," she explained most adults' disinterest:

> For fantasy is true, of course. It isn't factual, but it is true. Children know that. Adults know it too, and that is precisely why many of them are afraid of fantasy. They know that its truth challenges, even threatens, all that is false, all that is phony, unnecessary, and trivial in the life they have let themselves be forced into living. They are afraid of dragons, because they are afraid of freedom.[2]

By avoiding high school, Christopher Paolini avoided other teenagers' aggressive rejection of fantasy just as he was embracing it. "If I had attended public school," he told Lieraturschock, "I have no doubt *Eragon* would not exist."[3] In fact, he believes a major advantage "to being homeschooled is you don't have the experience of being ridiculed or made fun of for who you are and what you're interested in. You never learn to be afraid to pursue your own interests."[4]

After earning a high school diploma from the American School in Chicago, Illinois (an accredited correspondence school), Paolini told *USA Today*, "I didn't have a lot to do. Dad felt I was too young to go to college; I didn't have a job, and the nearest town was some 20 miles away. I needed a way of entertaining myself. Writing was what I settled on."[5]

Not having to go to school or earn a living set Christopher apart from many writers. He seemed the happier for it.

Did you know...

Since its founding in 1897, the American School in Chicago, Illinois, has admitted an estimated three million students from across the country. Offering courses from accounting to writing, the school is accredited by the North Central Association of Colleges and Schools and is recognized by the Illinois State Board of Education as a secondary school. Tuition for its 18-credit unit college preparatory course is less than $1,500; graduates of the program have been admitted to numerous respected universities. Because of the flexibility available to its students (who can do their work anytime and anywhere) the program has attracted a number of well-known students. Among them: Jessica Alba, Donny and Marie Osmond, Andre Agassi, and Anna Kournikova. The school's Web site describes Christopher Paolini as American School's "favorite author."*

***http://www.americanschoolofcorr.com/grads.asp.**

The freedom and time to create is something authors value tremendously. In her book *Writing Down the Bones*, Natalie Goldberg confessed:

> I feel very rich when I have time to write and very poor when I get a regular paycheck and no time to work at my real work. . . . We exchange our time in life for money. Writers stay with the first step—their time—and feel it is valuable even before they get money for it.[6]

OUTLINING A DRAGON

Christopher Paolini's novel began with extensive research. He relied on the Old Norse, German, Old English, and Russian languages for most of the names for his characters and places. Because he loved modern fantasy's inspirations—stories from Scandinavian, Old Norse, and Teutonic history, for example—he delved deeper into their origins.

Classical music provided more inspiration. As he wrote, he listened to the works of composers like Ludwig van Beethoven, Carl Orff, and Gustav Mahler. The primary "soundtrack" for his writing was Richard Wagner's Ring cycle of operas. Wagner was a German composer who had modest success before being forced to flee Dresden following a revolution in 1848. Settling in Switzerland, he focused on composing his masterwork, *Der Ring des Nibelungen* ("The Ring of the Nibelungen"), which was inspired by his love of Norse sagas. It consumed his creative life for the next 20 years. "Between 1850 and 1865 Wagner fashioned most of the material to which he owes his reputation," as quoted from the *Encyclopedia of World Biography*. "He purposefully turned aside from actual composition to plan an epic cycle of such grandeur and proportion as had never been created before."[7]

The entire Ring cycle first premiered in 1876, more than three decades after the idea had first come to mind. In it, Wagner "envisioned a world made entirely free from subservience to supernatural bondage, which he believed had adversely affected Western civilization from ancient Greece to the present," noted *World Biography*. He believed human activity was motivated by

> fear, which must be purged so that man can live the perfect life. In the *Ring* he attempted to set forth the standards for superior humans, those beings who would dominate individuals less fortunate; in turn, such lesser mortals would recognize their own inferior status and yield to the radiance offered by the perfect hero.[8]

The rustic landscape surrounding Paolini's home was also a profound influence upon his work. "The scenery here cannot be beat, and it's one of the main sources of inspiration for me," he admitted in an online interview conducted by David Weich of Powell's bookstore in Portland, Oregon. "I go hiking a lot, and oftentimes when I'm in the forest or in the mountains, sitting down and seeing some of those little details makes the difference between having an okay description and having a unique description."[9]

While learning what he wanted to write about, Paolini was also learning *how* to write. "Like so many homeschoolers, Christopher tackles projects by educating himself," explains the online article "Christopher Paolini and *Eragon*: A Homeschool Success Story."[10]

After so many abortive attempts at a novel, Christopher worked to ensure his next work had a beginning, a middle, and an end. Before earning a high school diploma, he had already earned college credits from correspondence writing courses. Still, books remained his best resource. "Before I started," he told *The Writer* magazine, "I studied books on stories and characters and plots. One was *The Writer's Handbook.* And *Story* by Robert McKee gave me an idea of story structure."[11] He explained, "Though *Story* is intended for screenwriters, I found McKee's principles and advice invaluable for structuring a novel."[12] He also made use of Orson Scott Card's book *Characters and Viewpoint*.

Paolini knew his novel would feature characters that were more romantic than realistic. On the one hand, romantic characters are often ones with abilities and with heroic traits beyond that of most readers; they usually reside in exotic locations. Realistic characters, on the other hand, live everyday lives readers are familiar with, although they often confront extraordinary situations.

In his book *On Writing*, Stephen King advised aspiring novelists:

> If you happen to be a science fiction fan, it's natural that you should want to write science fiction (and the more sf you've read, the less likely it is that you'll simply revisit the field's well-mined conventions . . .). If you're a mystery fan, you'll want to write mysteries, and if you enjoy romances, it's natural for you to want to write romances of your own.[13]

Paolini had loved the fantasy genre for years. He imagined a book he would want to read. Although the main character could have special abilities, he wanted him to

Christopher Paolini with a sample of the calligraphy he used for the books in his Inheritance series. While writing the first draft of the series, he often wrote on parchment with a quill pen.

also be familiar to readers like himself. He decided his protagonist, like himself, would be 15 years old. But he would also excel in magic and sword fighting. Paolini believed these skills, along with the story's benevolent dragon, exotic locations, and interesting characters, would inspire awe.

"If there is no awe, there is no audience," Card explained in *Characters and Viewpoint*.

> In every successful story—every story that is loved and admired by at least one reader who is not a close friend or a blood relative of the author—the author has created characters who somehow inspire enough admiration, respect, or awe that readers are willing to identify with them, to become their disciples for the duration of the tale.[14]

After reading books on writing and considering the type of story he wished to tell, Paolini recalled, "I spent an entire month to plot out *Eragon* and the two sequels. Many writers don't work this way. But for me, I figure out what I'm going to write beforehand, so I'm free to concentrate on presenting it in the most beautiful, eloquent manner possible."[15]

ERAGON

Stephen King once recalled being asked how he wrote his novels. "One word at a time," he told the interviewer. "I think he was trying to decide whether or not I was joking. I wasn't. . . . Whether it's a vignette of a single page or an epic trilogy like *The Lord of the Rings*, the work is always accomplished one word at time."[16]

During the winter in early 1999, Christopher Paolini opened a notebook and began writing the first words of what would be his Inheritance trilogy. The work eventually filled hundreds of pages.

He wrote wherever and however he could. He wrote in his notebook and on a sheet of parchment paper with a quill pen. He wrote in his bedroom and in the dimly lit study. Mainly he worked on the ancient couch in the living room, not far from the family's wood-burning stove.

As he began writing, he felt blessed. "Something a lot of people don't realize," he explained to BookBrowse, "is that in order to write a book, you have to have time. . . . I had time to just write."[17] Time, however, can also be an enemy. Unstructured days stretch before the writer. Those days might be filled with outlining or research or daydreaming but little actual writing. In a September 2003 interview, Christopher Paolini described the downfalls of having too much time:

> It's far too easy to get distracted from your work, or tire of it and find a simpler project. The true sign of a professional writer is that he or she can—and does—write every day, even without feeling inspired. Writing is not a gift from the gods. It does not spring fully formed from the author's brow. Writing is a craft, and, like any craft, you must practice, practice, practice to hone your skills. This can get boring if you feel that all you must do is connect with your muse and a new best-seller will flow forth. Alas, no. And even if you are a seasoned author and acclimated to the work of writing, it is still dangerously easy to become engaged in minor tasks that—like insidious, scaly carnivores—consume your precious minutes.[18]

He was not afraid of the ambitious project before him. Despite never finishing an entire novel, he created an outline that planned for him to write three of them. "I decided to make this one a trilogy," he explained to Teenreads.com.

> I like trilogies because they match the structure of a three-act play, and they appeal to my sense of symmetry. As I invented the world and events of the trilogy, I tried to imbue them with the elements I enjoy most in books: an intelligent, questioning hero; lavish descriptions; exotic locations; dragons; elves; dwarves; magic; and above all else, a sense of awe and wonder.[19]

Still, he admitted to having second thoughts in his interview with Bookbrowse. "In retrospect, it might not have been the wisest thing—undertaking such a huge project as my first book—but as they say, you can only learn through doing."[20]

Although his main character's name, Eragon, was simple (dragon with the first letter changed) and Paolini was committed to making sure most of Eragon's problems would be familiar, he also wanted the trials of this young farm boy to resonate with readers. The novel describes how Eragon finds, in the mountains, a mysterious stone, which is in fact an egg. A dragon he later names Saphira hatches from it.

Paolini realized that "when I'm writing if I happen to get sidetracked into long pastoral descriptions or too many fantastical elements, I find that my interest, even as the writer, diminishes," he admitted in an interview. "It doesn't return until somehow I find a way to get back to the characters' inner lives and how they're dealing with the questions of everyday life."[21] Yet even as he worked to maintain his protagonist's connection to everyday life, he was aware of his work's connection not

Swiss psychiatrist Carl Gustav Jung (1875–1961) is known as the founder of analytical psychology. Jung believed a collective unconscious existed among human beings that allowed them to form connections among universal images and symbols.

just to fantasy but also to stories that are thousands of years old.

JUNG, CAMPBELL, AND THE ARCHETYPE

Paolini was not alone in his fascination with ancient legends. "The great fantasies, myths and tales are indeed like dreams: they speak *from* the unconscious *to* the unconscious, in the *language* of the unconscious—symbol and archetype,"[22] Le Guin wrote in her book *The Language of the Night*. Two men who particularly examined the role of symbol and archetype in the twentieth century were Carl Jung and Joseph Campbell.

Carl Jung was a Swiss-born psychoanalyst. "While observing his patients Jung noticed that symbols occurring in their dreams sometimes caused highly emotional reactions," as quoted in *Scientists: Their Lives and Works*. After determining that the symbols had no real meaning for the patient, he realized, "many of the same symbols seem to reappear throughout history in religion, the arts, folktales, and other forms of human expression." Jung saw these constantly recurring symbols as part of the collective unconsciousness, "a cross-generational pool of inherited psychological associations that originated with the beginning of the human race. According to Jung, every human has access to the collective unconscious; common experiences, therefore, form universal images and mental connections in all people."[23]

An American mythologist, writer, and lecturer, Joseph Campbell, who helped to compile *The Portable Jung* in 1971, examined in his own writing the role of archetypes, which he believed to be vitally important to storytelling. "By its nature, fantasy draws upon archetypes," Liz Rosenberg of the *New York Times* commented, "less enchanted readers might call them stereotypes—of heroes and villains, magic and magical creatures."[24]

Figures like the dragon, the evil king, and the boy-warrior are all archetypes, characters that Campbell believed recur frequently enough to touch the unconscious memory and reappear continually in mythical tales. While living in Paris, Campbell was "influenced by the art of Pablo Picasso and Henri Matisse, the novels of James Joyce and Thomas Mann, and the psychological studies of Sigmund Freud and Carl Jung," according to the biographical section of Campbell's groundbreaking book *The Hero with a Thousand Faces*. "These encounters led to Campbell's theory that all myths and epics are linked in the human psyche, and that they are cultural manifestations of the universal need to explain social, cosmological, and spiritual realities."[25]

The "hero's journey" was an archetype Campbell examined in *The Hero with a Thousand Faces*, which is often cited as a template by novelists and screenwriters. In his book, Campbell explained, "A hero ventures forth from the world of common day into a region of supernatural wonder: fabulous forces are there encountered and a decisive victory is won: the hero comes back from this mysterious adventure with the power to bestow boons on his fellow man."[26] In works as diverse as *Beowulf*, *Star Wars*, *Rocky*, *Spider-Man*, and the Harry Potter novels, the main character has a goal, usually defined at the beginning of the tale. Over the course of the story, the main character, or hero, encounters numerous obstacles as he attempts to achieve his goal. While pursuing this singular ambition, and often without realizing it, the hero changes, usually maturing, and is different in the end.

Eragon, Christopher Paolini's first novel, is just such a hero's journey. For the author, his hero Eragon "started as me but ended up evolving into his very own character," he explained to *USA Today*. "Even as he has gone through his coming-of-age story, the process of writing and publishing these novels has been my own coming-of-age story. There are parallels between my own experience and Eragon's, but fortunately, I don't have people charging at me with swords."[27]

Taking the time to craft an outline proved beneficial. "I worked sporadically at first," he admitted to Teenreads.com, "but as I became more and more engaged with my project, I spent as much time as I could writing. The first 60 or so pages were written in longhand, until I learned how to type."[28]

Writing by hand at first and later composing on a Macintosh computer, Christopher Paolini disappeared into the world his imagination created. As he wrote, his sister and his parents were encouraging. Still, he wrote with the door shut, even when he was writing in the family living room. Following the lead of innumerable successful authors, Paolini kept what he was writing a secret and did not show the first draft to anyone.

The more he wrote, the easier it got. "*Eragon* flowed out of me at a tremendous pace; I never had writer's block. Part of my speed was due to the fact that I had no idea what, technically, constituted good writing, and therefore, I did not edit myself during this process."[29] By the end of 1999, Christopher Paolini had finished the first draft of *Eragon*. His family could not wait to read it. Instead of giving it to his family, however, he sat down and read the manuscript himself first.

After studying books on writing, outlining, and attempting to craft a hero's journey, Christopher Paolini had finally succeeded in writing a novel with a beginning, middle, and end. There was only one problem. He hated it.

A December 1955 photo of J.R.R. Tolkien (1892–1973), the British writer and professor, reading in his study at Oxford University. Tolkien's fantasy masterworks, The Hobbit *and* The Lord of the Rings, *were an enormous inspiration to Christopher Paolini.*

4

Revision

IN THE NOVEL *Eragon*, the main character's uncle Garrow gives him the following advice:

> Let no one rule your mind or body. Take special care that your thoughts remain unfettered. One may be a free man and yet be bound tighter than a slave. Give men your ear, but not your heart. Show respect for those in power, but don't follow them blindly. Judge with logic and reason but comment not. Consider none your superior, whatever their rank or station in life.[1]

This is bold advice to give to an unlikely hero. Eragon—a poor farm boy being raised by his uncle—seemed to have no special destiny. Then while hunting one day, Eragon discovered a blue dragon's egg. Dragons decide for whom they hatch, often remaining in their egg for years. They wait for their "Riders."

Saphira hatches for Eragon. She believes he has the talents to become a Rider, one of a class of special warriors who possess fighting ability and skills with magic, and are linked mentally to their dragons. When Riders ruled the world, citizens were freer. Once numerous, Riders are nearly extinct by the time Eragon is 15 years old. One of the last Riders, in fact, had used his abilities to gain power—the corrupt and dangerous King Galbatorix.

Accompanied by a former Rider named Brom, Eragon barely escapes the farm after Galbatorix's minions torture and murder his uncle. Eragon learns he is considered the best hope not just for humans but for the dwarves and elves of his country as well. His dragon comforts him by reminding him of his destiny. "Every age needs an icon. . . . Farm boys are not named for the first Rider without cause," Saphira tells Eragon. "Your namesake was the beginning, and now you are the continuation. Or the end."[2]

REVISING THE NOVEL

This was the story Christopher Paolini wanted to tell. Yet, he knew what he had written needed some serious revision. In an interview, he remembered:

> By the end of 1999, I had completed the first draft of *Eragon*. At last I was able to read my own book from start to finish . . . and I was dismayed by how amateurish it seemed. The story was fine, but it was mired in atrocious language and grammar. I was like a musician who has composed his first aria, only to discover that he can't perform it because he has not yet learned

> to sing. I set out to rewrite *Eragon* with the goal of raising the language to a professional level.[3]

He had written an adventure, a fantasy story in a land of his own creation with inspirations from imaginary places like J.R.R. Tolkien's Middle-earth. He admitted the story arrived in a "gigantic burst" and that the result was raw and uncontrolled. After a year of work, he was unwilling to show the first draft of his novel to anyone—just as many other authors are. While writing the first draft of any work, Stephen King advised:

> There may come a point when you want to show what you're doing to a close friend . . . either because you're proud of what you're doing or because you're doubtful about it. My best advice is to resist this impulse. . . . If you have someone who has been impatiently waiting to read your novel . . . then this is the time to give up the goods . . . if, that is, your first reader or readers will promise not to talk to you about the book until *you* are ready to talk to *them* about it.[4]

For Christopher, there were at least two people eager to see what he had been spending the last year working on: his mother and father. They were more understanding than most; it is hard to imagine the average parent being excited that their teenage son, without paycheck or school schedule, devoted a solid year to writing a dragon story. Talita Paolini continued to encourage him during the revision process. "She regards her son's book as a natural extension of his home schooling," one reporter explained.[5] Although his sister read Christopher's outline, he was not ready to share the novel with Angela either.

Instead, he spent the next year revising. Many believe the difference between an amateur writer and a professional is that the latter understands revision's necessity. Paolini admitted, "I don't think anyone would read authors' books if we weren't able to rewrite."[6]

In her book on writing, *Bird by Bird*, Anne Lamott noted:

> People tend to look at successful writers . . . and think that they sit down at their desks every morning . . . feeling great about who they are and how much talent they have and what a great story they have to tell; that they take in a few deep breaths, push back their sleeves, roll their necks a few times to get all the cricks out, and dive in, typing fully formed passages as fast as a court reporter. But this is just the fantasy of the uninitiated. I know some very great writers, writers you love who write beautifully and have made a great deal of money, and not *one* of them sits down routinely feeling wildly enthusiastic and confident. Not one of them writes elegant first drafts.[7]

The process of rewriting was radically different. "Once my first draft of *Eragon* was finished," he told Bookbrowse, "I had to learn how to write properly. . . . The first step in writing my book was a purely creative phase. After that, however, came the grind of editing the manuscript into readable material."[8]

Christopher spent the next twelve months revising his rough first draft. "My second draft—which took a second year (2000)—was larger than the first and bloated with far too many words,"[9] he recalled. After two years of work, it was time for him to open the door and let everyone see what he had written. "At that point," he remembered, "I turned the manuscript over to my parents, both of whom are published authors."[10]

Their initial response was enthusiastic. Even his father, Kenneth Paolini, liked it—and the elder Paolini did not like fantasy. "My parents read it and thought it was great," he told a reporter from the *Telegraph*. "But I didn't really trust their opinion. After all, they're my parents. I wasn't surprised they liked it."[11]

Then they did surprise him. They wanted to publish it. It would be a family project, with family money. Christopher wrote the novel alone. It would succeed, or fail, with the help of his sister, his mother, and his father.

FANTASY HISTORY

By the time Christopher Paolini was old enough to drive a car, not only had he read hundreds of fantasy novels, he had also written one. It was no accident that his first novel would be written in this genre. "It's hard to attribute the success of science fiction and fantasy to any one element," the author told Teenreads.com. "Both genres are far too diverse to be able to point to just one thing and say, 'This is why people love these books.' "[12]

While science fiction captures a human desire to imagine the future, fantasy "is the language we first learn," explained fantasy author Nancy Varian Berberick. "Christian, Jew or Buddhist, whatever, it is the language of our religions. What is faith but the ability to imagine the fantastic and choose to believe in it?"[13] Yet Berberick does not feel that fantasy is limited to the young: "One learns best in one's native tongue, and fantasy is the language I learned in childhood. Life's lessons, hard and adult, are still, for me, most easily learned in that language."[14]

The fantasy subgenre Paolini was writing in is known as "sword and sorcery." It traces its popularity to the Conan the Barbarian character created by Robert E. Howard in a series of novels first published in the 1930s. In his essay,

A 2005 photo of Christopher Paolini, author of the best-selling fantasy novels* Eragon *and* Eldest*, in Montana. The big skies, mountains, and wide-open spaces of his home state helped to inspire the imaginary fantasy world of his novels.

"Sword and Sorcery, Dragon and Princess," Darrell Schweitzer explained:

> The sword and sorcery story depends on three elements, which *must* be in every story: 1) an imaginary, pregunpowder setting, usually based on medieval or ancient societies; 2) magic; and 3) a vigorous heroic warrior as a central character. He or she *must* be a warrior. You could have a story about magic and

> imaginary lands in which the protagonist is a shoemaker, but while that would be fantasy, it wouldn't be what most readers and editors mean by *sword* and *sorcery*.[15]

Growing up in the isolated country, Paolini was often able to let his imagination reach out in all directions. For him—and he believes, for most people—fantasy and science fiction are a part of imagination's natural extension. As he ascended Emigrant Mountain, he imagined climbing not by foot, but saddled to a flying dragon. He pictured the Bear Tooth Range 10 times taller; he envisioned the land surrounding Yosemite as a region beset by dangerous shades and ruled for over a century by a malevolent king. This land of his imagination he would call Alagaësia.

"I believe that a large part of [fantasy and science fiction's] appeal comes from the exercise of pure imagination and flights of fancy, as well as the intellectual delight of attempting to extrapolate the evolution of technology," the teen novelist later explained. "I enjoy fantasy because it allows me to visit lands that have never existed . . . to experience daring adventures with interesting characters, and, most importantly, to feel the sense of magic in the world."[16] In an interview with *The Writer*, he remarked that "fantasy combines [adventure] with mythic elements to create a sense of awe and wonder, that sense of magic in the world. And the style of writing is different than in everyday speech. The language of fantasy is very beautiful."[17]

It is also a challenge. Ursula K. Le Guin has objected to the kind of commonplace everyday language that is found in some fantasy novels, but noted:

> [T]he archaic manner, which [Lord] Dunsany and other master fantasists use so effortlessly . . . is a trap into which almost

> all very young fantasy writers walk. . . . They know instinctively that what is wanted in fantasy is a *distancing from the ordinary*. They see it done beautifully in old books, such as Malory's *Morte d'Arthur* . . . and they think, "Aha! I will do it too."[18]

Yet for the novice writer, the choice between an archaic manner of speaking and a style of conversational language, which Le Guin derides as "journalistic," leaves the creator failing in terms of style. Failing stylistically is a greater failure in fantasy than in any other type of fiction, she believes, because "in fantasy there is nothing but the writer's vision of the world. . . . A world where no voice has ever spoken before; where the act of speech is the act

Did you know...

Although there had been earlier works of fantasy and science fiction, films and books in this genre gained an enormous following beginning in the 1950s. Noted sci-fi author Orson Scott Card listed his favorite books from his youth in the 1960s:

1. **Robert A. Heinlein, *Citizen of the Galaxy***
2. **Andre Norton, *The Stars are Ours***
3. **Robert A. Heinlein, *Tunnel in the Sky***
4. **Andre Norton, *Galactic Derelict***
5. **Andre Norton *Catseye****

***Source: Darrell Schweitzer, "The Top Ten Favorites List," *How to Write Tales of Horror, Fantasy & Science Fiction*, J.N. Williamson, ed. Cincinnati: Writer's Digest Books, 1987, p. 192.**

of creation. The only voice that speaks there is the creator's voice. And every word counts."[19]

Paolini's literary influences inspired the language he used to write his novel. One writer called *Eragon* "an adventure fantasy in the familiar mould of Tolkien's *Lord of the Rings*, with nods to Thomas Malory's *Morte d'Arthur*, Wagner's 'Ring Cycle,' and a clutch of popular children's books, including *Jeremy Thatcher, Dragon Hatcher*."[20]

After a second year of revisions, the budding author finally enlisted his parents' help. Not only did they assist him with editing, they would pay for the book's publishing costs. As he noted in one interview, "My parents and I had decided to self-publish *Eragon* for financial and creative reasons."[21] The creative control, however, also meant the family could be saddled with piles of unsold books and unpaid debt.

A photo of the Reed College campus in Portland, Oregon. Christopher Paolini debated about attending school here before devoting himself (with his parents' blessing) full-time to his writing.

5

Storyteller

WRITERS USUALLY BEGIN their books alone. Anyone who hopes to become a published author, however, must accept collaboration. Agents and editors usually offer their opinions on how the work can be improved. The wise writer at least considers every suggestion and tries to incorporate as many as possible without radically altering his or her original vision. In Christopher Paolini's case, he had an unusual situation. He lived with his editors. "The real torture with *Eragon* came in the editing," Paolini confessed in an interview with Teenreads.com. Describing his third year of work on *Eragon*, he explained, "I discovered that editing is really another word for someone ruthlessly tearing apart your work with a big smile, all the while telling you that it will make the book so much better. And it did, though it felt like splinters of hot bamboo being driven into my tender eyeballs."[1]

Angela helped her brother create languages for *Eragon*'s Urgals, elves, and dwarves. He rewarded her by putting his sister "in the book as a character, Angela the Herbalist," he later told *Time for Kids*. "Fortunately, my sister has a good sense of humor. I originally put her in as a joke. . . . It's

Did you know...

In 2003, Angela Paolini mentioned her own novel in a newspaper article: "I will be releasing it to Mom and Dad sometime soon."* Since that time there has been little information on this work, although Angela's name is mentioned on many Web sites in connection with her brother. Even if her novel is eventually published, matching her brother's success would be a challenge.

Perhaps the best-known sibling authors are the Brontë sisters. Although Charlotte Brontë's novel *Jane Eyre* was a literary success when it was published in 1847, her sister Emily's *Wuthering Heights*, published the same year, failed to sell. The latter novel would not receive acclaim until some time after Emily Brontë's death.

*Source: Dinitia Smith, "Finding a Middle Earth in Montana; A Teenager's Fantasy Set in a Magical Land Is a Best Seller," *New York Times*, October 7, 2003, p. E1.

hard having someone else write what they think you're like in a book. But she retaliated. She just finished up her first book and she put me in it."[2]

While Christopher's sister and mother line-edited *Eragon*, his father typeset the corrected pages on his computer using Adobe PageMaker. Publishing the novel themselves, however, did not guarantee its success. In fact, self-published books were once scorned by editors and agents as the products of hack writers who were unable to interest legitimate publishing houses in their works. Today, however, attitudes toward such books are evolving. After all, many books published by major houses began their life as self-published titles. For example, Lisa Genova spent 18 months trying to find a literary agent to represent her novel about a Harvard professor battling Alzheimer's disease. Despite sending dozens of letters to agencies, only four asked to see the complete manuscript. None of them felt it would sell to a major publishing house. Genova decided to publish it herself. "Don't do that," one of the agents who had read the book cautioned, "you'll kill your writing career before it starts."[3]

He was wrong. Instead, as a self-published novel through iUniverse, *Still Alice* earned a glowing review from the *Boston Globe* and later won a contract with a major publisher, Simon & Schuster. Ultimately, it appeared atop several best-seller lists. "If you believe in your book, I think you should give it a chance," Genova now advises aspiring authors.[4]

PREPARING THE FIRST EDITION

The Paolinis were going to give *Eragon* that chance. In order to do so, Kenneth Paolini even set up a new company imprint, Paolini International LLC. But the author had his own work to do. "As if writing around 500 pages about a 15-year-old who discovers a dragon's egg wasn't enough," the *Christian Science Monitor* reported, "[Christopher] Paolini designed the cover art and drew the illustrated map of his kingdom."[5] "Between drafts," Paolini added, "I had illustrated the original book cover and drew the interior maps and a self-portrait for the back cover." He also worked on a glossary to provide a pronunciation guide for characters' names as well as words in "The Ancient Language," along with words in the languages of dwarves and Urgals.[6]

While crafting new material, Paolini endured changes his parents and sister made to the old. Lengthy descriptions and anachronistic words that would seem odd to modern-century readers were often eliminated. Later he admitted with some pleasure that a few words like "sward"—a Middle English word meaning land covered with grass—were retained. He preferred to keep antiquated language because he often felt that the English used in the twenty-first century could be disappointing. "I was looking recently in a few supposedly very comprehensive thesauruses and I was dismayed by how pale and wan the language was in these thesauruses," he admitted to Powells.com. "They seemed to be lacking a lot of the richness. And I was able to find in an ancient thesaurus dating from the early nineteen hundreds words in there you cannot find anywhere else."[7]

Working toward a completed novel that people might pay to read took a great deal of time. Although it was difficult—and sometimes even painful—he learned, like his hero Eragon, to appreciate the journey. "Editing and revision are two of the most important tools for forging a great book," he explained to Teenreads.com. "With my parents' advice, I was able to clarify my descriptions, streamline my logic, and quicken the pace of the story so that *Eragon* read the way that I had intended it to. This consumed the bulk of 2001."[8]

The Paolini family had expended considerable time and money on Christopher's dream. By the middle of 2001, the teenager found himself struggling with a decision—whether to replace his dream of becoming an author with a more conventional ambition.

HIGHER EDUCATION

Two years after earning his high school diploma, Christopher Paolini was curious about college. He was almost 18 and had never really been in a classroom. Nor had he ever spent any significant time away from his family. The idea of going to college was both exciting and scary.

He applied to a university known for its nontraditional curriculum. Located in a southeast Portland neighborhood, Reed College was founded in 1908 and named for Oregon pioneers Simeon and Amanda Reed. According to its Web site,

> [Reed College] has remained steadfast to one central commitment: to provide a balanced, comprehensive education in liberal arts and sciences, fulfilling the highest standards of intellectual excellence. The distinctive Reed experience includes a challenging curriculum involving wide reading, conference and laboratory-based teaching in small groups, and a student body motivated by enthusiasm for serious intellectual work. . . . The curriculum at Reed is highly structured and extremely rigorous.[9]

Reed College also feels "The balance of a general and more specialized education is best achieved where students and faculty members work closely together in an atmosphere of shared intellectual and scholarly concern."[10]

For a homeschooled student, he was excited by the prospect of joining a "larger intellectual life." When Paolini received an acceptance letter in the summer of 2001, he also learned he had earned a full scholarship. Despite this, he decided not to attend. After spending more than two years working on his novel, he did not want to leave Montana before his family published it. "If I had gone I wouldn't have been able to promote *Eragon*."[11]

Instead, he spent the rest of the year completing his final draft of the book. He later explained:

> Near the end of 2001, my dad formatted the book in Adobe PageMaker for publication. He determined how wide the text block would be, how much space would occupy the top and bottom of the pages, what the chapter titles should look like, how the cover should be designed, and much, much more. While he did that, my mom and I prepared promotional materials for book signings and other events.[12]

The last of the family's savings went into publishing the book. Although it was Print-on-Demand, meaning they only had to produce a book when it was ordered, Kenneth Paolini wanted to ensure that potential customers could purchase the book immediately, so he spent thousands of dollars on the first shipment. "People told us we were nuts to do this," the elder Paolini remembered. "So what else is new?"[13]

After convincing a number of local bookstore managers and owners to allow a self-published teenager to market his novel in their store, Christopher Paolini dressed in medieval costume (his mother's idea) and the rest of the family would set up a table, laden with fresh copies of *Eragon*. "I would talk to every single person who would come in the door of the book store for usually eight or nine hours straight and I would not leave the table the whole time," the author told the *Courier Mail*. "I would try to sell every single person a book."[14]

The dream was no longer his alone. "One reason I worked so intensely at this was my family had put their personal finances into getting the book off the ground," he later admitted. "My parents weren't working at anything else at that time so books sold meant food on the table, so as I result I learnt how to sell the book. I actually sold the book once to a man who didn't even read English."[15]

Doing better than most self-published authors, Christopher Paolini usually sold several dozen copies with each store visit. Yet it was not enough. After setting up at every local store that would have them, the Paolinis had to drive farther and farther to find untapped markets. This consumed their profits. "This support was a continuation of my parents' homeschooling philosophy, to nurture my interests, and through those interests help me learn and mature," he later explained to German Web site Literaturschock.[16]

The family brainstormed ways to sell more books. Even successful bookstores do not attract as many young readers as the average junior high, so they decided to go to schools. "We took it around the local libraries and schools, and then Dad had this idea for marketing it," he told a reporter. "We worked out a show, with me dressed up in my armor, and I took it around schools and read from the book. We drove as far as Texas one time, and I did hundreds of readings."[17] "Even though I was homeschooled," he told a reporter for *Time*, "I have been in more schools now than any person should ever be forced to go into. And I did do most of those events in medieval costume."[18]

One reporter asked if he ever felt self-conscious. "Not a bit," Christopher Paolini explained. "It attracted a lot of attention and people wanted to know more about the book. They would buy copies and I would sign them with my tag line, 'May your swords stay sharp.' "[19] They also traveled to small towns that had never hosted a writer, self-published or otherwise. "We went to places that never had an author," he explained to the *New York Times*, "places hungry for this."[20]

Eventually Christopher gave over 150 presentations of his show, "Why Read, Why Write?" The strategy succeeded. *Eragon*'s sales increased tenfold. It sometimes sold as many as 400 copies in a single day (with a student price of $14; $22.95 retail). Eventually the book sold more than 10,000 copies, an incredible accomplishment for a self-published title. Yet the effort was exhausting. "Our house was filled with copies of *Eragon*," Angela remembered. "They were stacked everywhere. We couldn't handle the demand."[21]

Despite its impressive name, Paolini International LLC was just a family publisher. "It was just way too much work for two adults and two teenagers,"[22] Paolini later noted. Taxed to their limits, the family found an unlikely savior.

CARL HIAASEN

Carl Hiaasen had begun his writing career working for a newspaper. Two years after graduating college, he was hired by the *Miami Herald* as a reporter. He had grown up in Florida at a time when the Everglades were primarily undeveloped swampland, and so his newspaper stories examined the impact of shopping centers and housing tracts in places like the Everglades. His nonfiction books often criticized corporations, most notably in his book *Team Rodent: How Disney Devours the World*. "Hiaasen wastes no time," explained one reviewer. "He sets his tone to rapid-fire acerbic, squeezes off a few rounds to clear his muzzle, then goes on full automatic, like Rambo taking on the world."[23] Beginning with 1986's *Tourist Season*, his novels addressed environmental concerns as well, with tongue-in-cheek descriptions and a cast of outlandish eccentrics. (His fiction, for example, includes an ex-governor who lives as a hermit and a hit man who replaced his amputated arm with a Weed Whacker.)

After his stepson and younger relatives complained he did not write books they could read, Hiaasen wrote his first young adult novel, *Hoot*, in 2002. The book not only found an audience, it also won a prestigious Newbery Medal and was later made into a movie.

The Paolinis' work and Hiaasen's life intersected during the novelist's trip to Montana. Seeking a diversion for his stepson during long hours of driving, he bought *Eragon* in a chain grocery store. Hiaasen was surprised to find it was self-published, but even more surprised when his stepson could not put it down.

Hiaasen took a look and quickly agreed with his stepson, who thought it was better than the Harry Potter series. The novelist did more than enjoy the book—he sent it to his editor at Knopf, the publisher of *Hoot*, in New York. At Knopf, Michelle Frey, like most editors, was on the lookout for the next big thing, especially something by an unknown author that could attract millions of readers. Reading *Eragon*, Frey believed she had found it.

Across the country, the Paolini family was at Seattle's Bookfest promoting the novel. When Frey reached them, they had no idea how a New York City publisher could have heard of *Eragon*. "We didn't even know what [Hiaasen] had done until a few weeks ago," Christopher Paolini admitted in a December 2003 interview. "But he changed our lives forever. It made all the difference to get the support of someone like that."[24]

Delivering *Eragon* to a major publisher meant more money and a wider audience for the book. It also meant the family home would no longer double as a book warehouse. The Paolinis were cautious, despite their enthusiasm. "We may live out in the middle of nowhere," Kenneth Paolini later explained to a reporter, "but we didn't fall off the turnip truck yesterday."[25]

The work that had begun as a 15-year-old boy's attempt at a novel had morphed into a family business. Any publishing deal would also involve the family.

Christopher Paolini's novel Eragon *was just the first book in his Inheritance series. Pictured above, the cover of* Eldest, *the second novel in the series, which was first published in 2005.*

6

Celebrity

KENNETH PAOLINI SEARCHED the Internet. He hoped to find an agent who could get his son—his whole family, in fact—the most favorable book deal. "We are operating a family business," he later told a reporter, "and we will all share in the proceeds."[1]

He found representation through an online chat group. Writers House, a top New York agency, counts among its clients Ken Follett, author of *World Without End*; Nora Roberts, author of *Angels Fall*; Michael Lewis, author of *Moneyball*; and Stephenie Meyer, author of the Twilight series.

Since a top publisher was already hoping to buy *Eragon*, attracting an agent's interest was fairly straightforward. (Typically, a first-time author must have an agent prior to contacting a publisher.) Still, Writers House agent Simon Lipskar earned the family's respect. Christopher Paolini has since dubbed him the "Comma Master." Writing in an acknowledgement, he complimented Lipskar as the one who "makes all things possible," along with "his brave assistant Daniel Lazar, who keeps the Comma Master from being buried alive underneath a pile of unsolicited [unasked for] manuscripts, many of which I fear are the result of *Eragon*."[2]

Christopher Paolini was still a teenager when his family agreed to a book contract with Alfred A. Knopf. *Eragon* earned a six-figure advance and a royalty structure superior to that given to most first-time novelists because, unlike most first novels, *Eragon* already had a track record.

"It was my own epic quest," Paolini confessed. "That's what it felt like at times. It's a great story after the fact but when you're living it and you're feeling it, it can be pretty dreadful because we had no guarantee any of this would work out properly so I'm grateful every single day that it did turn out well."[3]

After the contract was signed, Paolini again faced an experience he once called worse than fighting the evil Shades: editing. The expectations of a major publishing house—and Alfred A. Knopf's executive editor Michelle Frey in particular—were even higher than his mother's. After another round of editing, *Eragon* was shortened by 20,000 words (approximately 50 pages). The map Paolini created survived, but his depiction of the Dragon Saphira, which had adorned the cover, was moved inside the book. A professional illustrator named John Jude Palencar created *Eragon*'s new cover.

Before its publication, *Eragon* was distributed to more than 3,000 reviewers and organizations like the American Library Association (ALA). According to Knopf's director of publicity, the response was huge. When Knopf published the book in August 2003, it was an immediate sensation. Following a first printing of 100,000, more than 200,000 more copies would be printed in the next six weeks. Even that did not keep up with demand.

Did you know...

A number of books originally published for young adult readers have been "repackaged" for adults. While the contents remain the same, books such as Christopher Paolini's *Eragon*, Lois Lowry's *The Giver*, J.K. Rowling's Harry Potter series, Stephenie Meyer's Twilight series, and numerous others, have had their covers changed and sizes altered before being placed on adult bookracks. In fact, the trend extends back to noted science fiction and fantasy author Andre Norton as well. In the 1950s, an editor at Ace Books republished her hardcover books, which had been written for juveniles, as paperbacks with new titles and identical contents. The strategy led to sales over the one million mark and gave Norton her first bestseller.

The account of a homeschooled teen's self-published epic and its discovery by a best-selling writer garnered enormous publicity, but it was the story itself that found an eager audience. Like Carl Hiaasen's stepson, most young readers could not put it down. It was quickly compared to another successful novel featuring a young boy's quest to discover his own supernatural abilities. "Any kind of comparison to *Harry Potter* and J.K. Rowling is unfair," offered Barnes and Noble book buyer Joe Monti. "[Paolini] has his own little halo and glamour separate from Rowling."[4]

Eragon debuted at number three on the prestigious *New York Times* best-seller list. It quickly reached the top spot on other lists, including *USA Today*'s and the *Wall Street Journal*'s. It even supplanted *Harry Potter and the Order of the Phoenix* at number one on the *New York Times* list for best-selling fiction. In fact, *Eragon* remained on the list of best-selling fiction titles in the United States for more than 80 weeks. Nearly three million copies would be printed in America alone. While these are terrific numbers for an established novelist, they are absolutely extraordinary for a first-timer. The book also earned some 50 foreign language licenses, giving publishers across the globe the right to translate and publish *Eragon*.

"If I wrote a book where what's happened to me happened to a character, no one would believe it," Paolini explained to Jay MacDonald.

> People would literally say, where's the downside? Where's the conflict? There's nothing bad happening in this story! Fortunately, I've had my parents here to help not only keep the home environment safe and sheltered but also help deal with all the publicity and attention that comes with it.[5]

That safe, sheltered feeling was going to be compromised. Christopher Paolini was about to embark on a book tour.

BOOK TOUR

The world of writers and readers is a solitary one. Novels are usually composed alone. The most successful of authors regularly confront the blank screen or page. The book tour alters those dynamics. It is a communal experience: Writers read from their latest works, sign autographs, and answer readers' questions.

Unlike movie stars, famous novelists are rarely recognized in public, even though they might earn millions of dollars and possess household names. "Christopher Paolini looks a little like Harry Potter," offered *USA Today*'s Carol Memmott, reporting on an author event Paolini attended. Describing his glasses, slight build, and a face that looked far younger than his years, she went on to note how "Paolini is recognized by only a handful of fans as he walks through the Barnes & Noble bookstore." More than 2,000 fans awaited his appearance, she reported, and "When he's finally introduced, he's treated like a rock star."[6]

Like rock stars, writers must cope with jet lag and missed airline connections, noisy hotel rooms, and weeks away from home's comforts. *The Writer* described Paolini's experience as "an exhausting 30-city book tour to promote *Eragon*."[7] Yet it had its comforts. He replaced his renaissance storyteller outfits with T-shirts and jeans. "It would take an act of God to get me back in that costume," Paolini admitted. "I don't need to fight for attention anymore."[8] Instead of convincing handfuls of students to buy his self-published novel, Paolini was now being mobbed by fans

On September 10, 2005, Christopher Paolini, then 21, signs his new novel, Eldest, *for a young fan during a promotional appearance in Kansas City, Missouri. This book tour was a far cry from the one he embarked on with his parents when they were hawking his self-published first novel from town to town.*

seeking his autograph. "You would not believe the things I've signed," he told one writer, "pretty much every outer article of clothing you can imagine—coats, hats, socks, shoes."[9]

Publishing success helped Paolini meet some of his literary heroes, including Bruce Coville, whose novel *Jeremy Thatcher, Dragon Hatcher* had inspired him as a 12-year-old to imagine dragons roaming Paradise Valley. Because his novel has sold millions of copies, Paolini admitted to the *Courier Mail* in the fall of 2008:

> My lifestyle has changed in some regard. I obviously travel now and go around the world and I spend more time writing than I used to, but for the most part our lives are still pretty sedate at home, which is nice. I go back home and I write and I still have to wash the dishes and vacuum the carpet and scrub the floor.[10]

EVERYONE'S A CRITIC

Being a best-selling novelist was not just about going on book tours and earning large advances. It also meant receiving reviews—lots of them. Even when it was a self-published book selling in the thousands, not the millions, *Eragon* had earned reviews. The number of reviews increased exponentially after the book became a bestseller. "I read reviews of my work, although sometimes I wish that I hadn't, even when it is a good review!" he explained to Teenreads.com. "Because everyone thinks about your work in a slightly different way, and if their views don't correspond with yours, it can be unsettling to see how your writing is interpreted."[11]

"Some writers, like Ursula K. Le Guin and Anne McCaffrey, use exquisite prose," noted Liz Rosenberg in a *New York Times* review. "Others, like J.R.R. Tolkien and J.K. Rowling, create reverberating plots that twist and dive with a dramatic flexibility that is like swordsmanship or dance. Paolini does not yet have these strengths."[12]

Still, despite Rosenberg's criticisms of *Eragon*'s "clichéd descriptions," "B-movie dialogue," "prose [that] can be awkward and gangly," and a "plot [that] stumbles and jerks along, with gaps in logic and characters dropped, then suddenly remembered, or new ones invented at the last minute," she found that "*Eragon*, for all its flaws, is an authentic work of great talent. . . . It never falters in its velocity. . . . I found myself dreaming about it at night, and reaching for it as soon as I woke."[13]

"In fantasy, if you have a character that's, say, afraid of spiders, they can run into a spider that's as large as a house," Paolini told *The Writer*. "It allows you to tailor the obstacles characters face specifically to their weaknesses."[14] Not all reviewers saw it this way. "Sometimes the magic solutions are just too convenient for getting out of difficult solutions," criticized *School Library Journal*.[15]

Criticism affected how the novice novelist wrote. "It can even make you change your writing style in an attempt to emphasize the elements that you think readers have ignored," Paolini admitted. "Despite this, I continue to read reviews because I believe that it's important to know how people are affected by *Eragon*, because I sometimes learn something valuable about my writing."[16]

Although Paolini had enjoyed the book tours, meeting fans, and reading favorable reviews, he realized the next part of his journey awaited. It was time to begin his second novel.

Many critics noted that Christopher Paolini's books bore some similarities to The Empire Strikes Back, *a 1980 film that was written by Leigh Brackett and Lawrence Kasdan, directed by Irvin Kerschner, and starred Mark Hamill (*pictured here*).*

7

Sequel

CHRISTOPHER PAOLINI HAD indeed come a long way—and in less time than it takes most teenagers to earn a college degree. In four years, he had gone from revising a book he was not very happy with to traveling across the country promoting a best-selling novel. In early 2004, he returned from the final leg of *Eragon*'s book tour in London, England, to the Montana house he grew up in.

Legally, Paolini was an adult. He was also a millionaire. Despite that, he was in little hurry to move out. "We like being together," the young novelist told a reporter with the London *Telegraph*. "If NASA is looking for a team of four people who can spend years with each other on a trip to Mars, we're it."[1] When the reporter, Michael Shelden, suggested the family spend some of their substantial earnings on a new house, Shelden wrote, "the entire Paolini clan . . . stare at me as though I wanted them to move to Las Vegas and take to drink." "It's our main stream of income," Angela noted. "We have to be careful how we spend it."[2]

Although *Eragon* had already sold millions of copies, the family realized there was no guarantee his next effort would match its success. Christopher Paolini was facing the dreaded "sophomore slump." The phrase refers to college students' challenges during their second year, rock stars' attempts to top their platinum-selling debut, and star rookie athletes' efforts to outdo their first season. The sophomore slump is a well-documented issue for many writers.

Unknown writers are truly able to shut the door. Their efforts are anonymous; aside from a few friends and family, no one cares. That changes after an aspiring author is published. If the novel succeeds, more people want to open that door. Reporters, bloggers, and casual readers all wonder about the next book. Major publishing houses hope to see a writer's second novel released within a year of the first. Besides the time an author spends promoting his first book, it takes time for the second one to be edited, printed, and promoted. Because of this, the length of time a writer has to finish his second novel is usually measured in months.

Fortunately, Christopher Paolini had already begun crafting the second book, which would be titled *Eldest*, in his carefully outlined trilogy. "In Book 2, I begin to explore Eragon's growing up," he explained to *The Writer*. "He's beginning to notice women. And how do you deal with that—when you're linked to a gigantic, scaly lizard who just happens to know your every thought? Their friendship [between the dragon Saphira and Eragon] is the core of the book."[3]

Paolini had learned from the intensive editing sessions he endured. Comparing the editing of his first novel to his second, he said it went "from intense to more intense," but admitted to interviewer Jay MacDonald, "I didn't make the same mistakes as I made in *Eragon*; I made entirely new mistakes."[4]

ELDEST

Returning to familiar territory is a challenge. How does an author keep his or her work fresh while following the same characters? "My first novel was a way to explore the standard fantasy traditions that I enjoyed reading so much," Paolini explained in an online interview with Powell's bookstore in Portland, Oregon. "It was a chance for me to play in this type of world. My second book and third book, as I see it, are opportunities to expand upon the original archetypes and try to bring a depth to the world that I haven't seen done or in ways that I want to explore personally."[5]

An archetype is "an original model or type after which similar things are patterned," wrote the author of *Understanding Movies*. "Archetypes can be well-known story patterns, universal experiences or personality types. Myths, fairy tales, genres, and cultural heroes are generally archetypal, as are the basic cycles of life and nature."[6]

Eldest was described by *Time* as "one of those tricky middle novels of a planned trilogy, a dark second act à la *The Empire Strikes Back*, full of reversals and repercussions and unexpected revelations."[7] In *The Empire Strikes Back*

(1980), the film sequel to *Star Wars* (1977), hero Luke Skywalker spends much of the film training to become a Jedi knight under the tutelage of an ancient Jedi master named Yoda before discovering that his greatest enemy, Darth Vader, is in fact his father.

Like Luke Skywalker, Eragon spends much of his time in *Eldest* training to be a Rider under the tutelage of the ancient elf Rider Oromis. Then, while Eragon is studying sword craft and magic, another story develops. After Eragon's older cousin Roran defends his village from Empire-led attacks, he takes most of the town's population on a countrywide pursuit of the evil Ra'zacs, who have kidnapped his fiancée.

"Eragon's growth and maturation throughout the book sort of mirrored my own growing abilities as a writer and as a person, too," he admitted in an interview. "In [*Eldest*], I switch viewpoint to Eragon's cousin, Roran. For a large part of the book, I'm flipping back and forth. That gave me the ability to move to a more mature character and explore some stuff I really can't deal with with Eragon at this point."[8]

REVIEWS AND CONTROVERSY

Multiple storylines and points of view were two reasons *Eldest* was nearly 700 pages long—200 pages longer than *Eragon*. Its length, along with the hundreds of pages devoted to Eragon's training with the elves, contributed to the book's mixed reviews following its North American release in August 2005. "I swear on Helzvog's stone girdle that I have not for many a year read anything so mind-numbingly silly as *Eldest*, the endless, overheated sequel to Christopher Paolini's best-selling 2003 *Lord of the Rings* knockoff, *Eragon*," Jennifer Reese began in her review in *Entertainment Weekly*. She later complained that "the sleazy political power struggle calls to mind another one of Paolini's debts: *Star Wars*."[9] Reese continued:

> Eragon and Saphira begin a pilgrimage to Ellesméra, the domain of the elf queen Islanzadí . . . [where] Eragon lives on honey cakes and thimbleberry jelly, and takes a crash course in magic and swordsmanship from the wise old elf Oromis. Malarkey like this might be forgiven if it were hitched to a fast-moving narrative. But Paolini dawdles, with long, self-indulgent asides about the proper components of a dwarfish bow (Feldûnost horns, skin from the roof of trout's mouths) and Eragon's romantic yearnings for emerald-eyed Arya.[10]

Although a critic for *Publishers Weekly* agreed with Reese that this "phone-book-size second helping in Paolini's planned Inheritance trilogy . . . sometimes seems less Tolkien than *Star Wars*," the reviewer concluded:

> [T]he most affecting element remains the tender relationship between dragon and Rider, and teens will empathize as the object of Eragon's affection (repeatedly) spurns him, his teacher humbles him and he struggles with questions about God and vegetarianism. Readers who persevere are rewarded with walloping revelations in the final pages, including the meaning of the title and the identity of the red dragon on the cover.[11]

Eldest was also more controversial than *Eragon* among some religious fans. When Oromis is asked by the book's hero what elves believe in, he admits that unlike dwarves and humans, elves do not worship a god or gods. "Be as that may," he adds, "I cannot prove that gods do *not* exist."[12] Yet in over a thousand years, Oromis admits elves

> have never witnessed an instance where the rules that govern the world have been broken. That is, we have never seen a miracle. . . . If gods exist, have they been good custodians of Alagaësia? Death, sickness, poverty, tyranny, and countless other miseries stalk the land. If this is the handiwork of divine beings, then they are to be rebelled against and overthrown, not given obeisance, obedience, and reverence.[13]

Reading passages like this, some Christians reacted with outrage. One blogger asked, "How dare Christopher Paolini drag out this atheist agenda in a children's book."[14]

Like many writers, Paolini asks that he not be judged by the actions or beliefs of his characters. "I don't discuss my own beliefs in public but I will say the beliefs I've given my characters do not necessarily represent what I myself believe," he told a reporter. "I try to create an interesting system of beliefs for all the different races and creatures within Eragon's world but whether or not that necessarily reflects my own views I'm not going to say. . . . The story should speak for itself to the reader."[15]

Although belief systems and vegetarian lifestyles discussed in *Eldest* do not necessarily reflect Paolini's own

Did you know...

Some of the languages *Eragon*, has been translated into include for example, Spanish, French, Swedish, Chinese, and Japanese.

practices, he incorporated his own experiences into his epic fairy tale. "One of the things I love about working on a large story is being able to fill it with interesting little tidbits from the world," he told Powell's. "For instance, puzzle rings. I came across them last year. . . . I gave one to my hero to stymie him."[16]

Uneven reviews and controversy did not seem to affect the book's sales; in financial terms *Eldest* was an unqualified success. Paolini's name returned to the number one spot on fiction best-seller lists. And as with his previous effort, Paolini's latest supplanted a book in the Harry Potter series, *Harry Potter and the Half-Blood Prince.* "In its first week on sale . . . [*Eldest*] sold more than 425,000 hardcover copies," Knopf's parent company, Random House, noted in a press release. This made *Eldest* "the greatest single-week sale ever recorded for a Random House Children's Books title, hardcover or paperback . . . [and] the fastest-selling title in the publisher's history."[17]

"When first I conceived *Eragon*, I was fifteen . . . just out of high school, unsure of what path to take in life, and addicted to the potent magic of the fantasy literature that adorned my shelves," Paolini wrote in *Eldest*'s acknowledgments. "The process of writing *Eragon*, marketing it across the world, and now finally completing *Eldest* has swept me into adulthood. I am twenty-one now and, to my continual astonishment, have already published two novels. Stranger things have occurred, I'm sure, but never to me."[18]

Christopher Paolini enjoyed his sophomore effort's financial success. With it, his family moved into a new house. And while he was promoting *Eldest*, film producers were busy developing *Eragon* into a movie—an adaptation the author and the producers hoped would be every bit as successful as the novel.

The poster art for the 2006 film adaptation of Eragon, *directed by Stefen Fangmeier. Many fans of Christopher Paolini's series—as well as most film critics—were disappointed by the movie.*

8

Eragon: The Motion Picture

ALL WRITERS HAVE influences. They are influenced by what they read, but also by the music they listen to, the movies and television programs they watch, even conversations they hear. Solitary observations from a sidewalk café have often had as great an impact on some novels as any work of literature. "Writing is a communal act," Natalie Goldberg asserted in *Writing Down the Bones*. "We are very arrogant to think we alone have a totally original mind. We are carried on the backs of all the writers who came before us."[1]

Christopher Paolini has been no different. He has traced *Eragon*'s origins to Norse mythology and *The Lord of the*

Rings, among many others. When the movie adaptation of his novel was released, however, many viewers and reviewers believed the film was in debt to one source above all others: the Star Wars movies. "*Eragon* is steeped in quotations: every ingredient, from dwarf to elf, from the brilliant blue stone of the dragon's egg to the old sage with the long white beard, is a stylised cliché," one critic noted. "Ask [Paolini] about *Eragon*'s villain, the wicked emperor Galbatorix, and he will cite Darth Vader of the Star Wars movies because, like him, Galbatorix started off "good"—a Dragon Rider—and turned to the dark side of fear and power."[2]

"Every so often a movie comes along that is so fresh, so complete in its artistic vision and captivating to movie goers that it simply stands apart from anything that has preceded it," asserted Eddie Dorman Kay in *Box Office Champs*. "D.W. Griffith's *Birth of a Nation* (1915) was such a film. So was David O. Selznick's *Gone with the Wind* (1939). And so too, was the box office champ for 1977, *Star Wars*, writer-director George Lucas's paean to the Flash-Gordon-Buck-Rogers sci-fi serials of his youth."[3]

Star Wars was more than a reflection of Lucas's childhood influences. Already a successful filmmaker, Lucas had helmed *American Graffiti*, which ranked tenth in the U.S. box office four years earlier, when he sought to film a modern-day epic of his own. While writing the screenplay for *Star Wars*, he was inspired by Joseph Campbell's book *The Hero with a Thousand Faces*, which greatly influenced the hero's journey in Lucas's script.

His film's main character, Luke Skywalker, is raised by an aunt and uncle, both of whom are murdered by foot soldiers from the Empire. He then befriends a hermit named Ben Kenobi, whom he later learns was once a Jedi Knight known as Obi-Wan Kenobi. The old master trains Luke in the Jedi practices, both mystical and physical. Although Kenobi is killed in a confrontation with his former pupil, Darth Vader, Luke is befriended by the guarded and cynical Han Solo, who helps him rescue Princess Leia, the woman whose secret tape led him to Kenobi. *Star Wars* concludes as Skywalker fights for the Jedis and hands the Empire one of its worst defeats.

When the film adaptation of *Eragon* debuted, critics pounced on the similarities between *Star Wars* and Paolini's first novel. *Eragon*'s protagonist is raised by his uncle, who is killed by foot soldiers for the Empire. Eragon befriends an eccentric local storyteller, Brom, who he later learns is a Dragon Rider. Brom trains Eragon in the ways of Dragon Riders, both mystical and physical. Although Brom is killed in a confrontation with Empire loyalists, Eragon continues on, aided by the guarded and cynical Murtagh. The two save the life of the elf Arya, who had transported the dragon egg to Eragon that led him to Brom and his journey as a Rider. In the novel's conclusion, Eragon fights for the Varden and hands the Empire one of its worst defeats.

MOVIE DREAMS

"Strangely enough, I actually imagined *Eragon* as a movie before I started writing it," he told a reporter at the movie's December 15, 2006, premiere party. "But since I didn't have the money that a studio has, I decided to make it a book instead. So to see *Eragon* now as a movie is almost like the culmination of this entire journey that began when I put pen to paper and wrote the first line in the book."[4]

Even as a 15-year-old aspiring novelist, Paolini recognized the enormous obstacles to filming his story. In order to accurately portray the dragon, along with an ancient setting populated by dwarves, elves, and Urdalls, it likely required an investment on the order of $100 million. As it turned out, the logistics of turning a novel like *Eragon* into a movie did require extensive preproduction. After optioning the novel for a film adaptation in February 2004, 20th Century Fox did not begin principal photography for nearly 18 months.

Following exhaustive location scouting, rural areas in the nations of Hungary and Slovakia stood in for Alagaësia. *Eragon* would be one of the biggest productions ever filmed in the two countries. During the summer of 2005, more than 500 members of the production crew descended upon the city of Budapest. Evil King Galbatorix's lair was built in a hillside cave—one only accessible through the roof. Equipment was lowered using special cranes.

Like its fictional inspiration, the film set for Farthen Dûr was constructed inside a dormant volcano. Formerly a rock quarry, it required four months of planning and construction. Since the battle scenes took place at night, Russian mountaineers were employed to lug up lighting equipment. Over several weeks of 10-hour days, some 450 extras and stunt people reenacted *Eragon*'s epic battle. Background performers portraying monstrous Urgals stood more than six-and-a-half feet tall while the ones playing dwarves were under five feet.

Creating the dragon was the production's most challenging element. Movies featuring dragons were regularly faulted for having either poor special effects or dragons that did not look like dragons. "This dragon looks more like a flying dog," a dragon fan said of the creature in the 1984 movie *The Neverending Story*.[5]

For the filmmakers, Saphira needed to be a fully realized character, not just an obviously computer-generated special effect. "Bringing Saphira to life was a huge undertaking that required my full attention and energies—much as a live action character requires the full attention of an actor," explained the movie's visual effects supervisor, Michael McAlister.

> There were thousands and thousands of specific decisions to be made in terms of how she would look, how she would act . . . and how she would fly. I did not invent her nor decide what her character would be, but I was responsible for understanding

Did you know...

Although portraying realistic-looking dragons in movies has always proven problematic, film companies have nevertheless repeatedly sought to do it. The Web site Draconian.com in its online article "Dragons of the Silver and Small Screen" lists a number of dragon-centric movies from the 1980s on, including *Reign of Fire*, *Dungeons and Dragons: The Movie*, *Dragonheart*, *Dragonheart: A New Beginning*, *Dragonslayer*, *Dragonworld*, *Quest for Camelot*, *Pete's Dragon*, *The Flight of Dragons*, *Mulan*, and *The Neverending Story*.

The Internet Movie Database (IMDB) Web site lists no fewer than 398 films with the keyword "dragon" in it, beginning with *Le Puits fantastique*, a 1903 short film, and including movies such as 1941's *The Reluctant Dragon*, 1981's *Excalibur* and *Dragon Riders of Pern*, which is listed as in development with a release date of 2011.

Author Christopher Paolini and his sister, Angela, arrive at the world premiere of Eragon *at Odeon Leicester Square in London, England, on December 11, 2006. Paolini had initially envisioned his fantasy epic as a movie.*

> her—inside and out—and deciding specifically how we would achieve her.[6]

Producers hired a professional screenwriter, Peter Buchman, despite Paolini's work on a screenplay. Having scripted special effects–driven movies like *Jurassic Park III*, Buchman described himself as "a fan of fantasy and science fiction literature and films." He also said he was "'blown away' by [Paolini's] precociousness, his mastery of plot lines and characters, and his ability to create several completely imaginary worlds."[7] "Christopher came up with this wonderful idea of a young man who develops a bond with a dragon," Buchman explained in a press release. "That relationship is at the core of the book, and that's what we had to translate to film."[8]

As each page of a script represents approximately one minute of screen time, Buchman had to condense the 500-page novel into a 120-page screenplay. Some reviewers found fault with this: "The challenge of paring down Paolini's massive tale to a manageable length results in slapdash pacing," commented Justin Chang when he reviewed the movie in *Variety*. "It takes all of five minutes for Eragon to get over the untimely death of his uncle Garrow (Alun Armstrong) and maybe five minutes more for his new pet to grow into an enormous, fully formed dragon named Saphira."[9]

Eragon's director, Stefen Fangmeier, a 1983 graduate of California State University of Dominguez Hills Computer Science program, had worked at George Lucas's Industrial Light and Magic (ILM) as a CG (Computer Generated) shot supervisor on *Terminator 2: Judgment Day* and a VFX (Visual Effects Supervisor) for *Twister*. His work has earned a British Academy of Film and Television Arts Award for

Saving Private Ryan, along with Academy Award nominations for *Ryan* and for *Master and Commander: The Far Side of the World*. He also worked as a second unit director on *Galaxy Quest* and *Dreamcatcher*, both complex jobs involving the supervision of numerous crewmembers.

Eragon was the first movie he directed. "With the book's fantastical aspects, people would look at me in terms of the visual effects requirements," he explained. "However, my first reaction to the material was that it was a great story that had an emotional arc."[10]

REVIEWS

When the film premiered in 2006, *Eragon* met with mixed reviews. A reviewer for the Hollywood trade paper *Variety* slammed both source material and adaptation:

> *Eragon* confirms that novelist Christopher Paolini is no J.R.R. Tolkien—but more to the point, helmer Stefen Fangmeier is no Peter Jackson [director of the movie adaptations of Tolkien's *The Lord of the Rings*]. Appropriating all the external trappings of big-budget fantasy but none of the requisite soul, this leaden epic never soars like the CG-rendered fire-breather at the core of its derivative mythology.[11]

Joe Morgenstern, a film critic for the *Wall Street Journal*, had a different opinion: "The film is the directorial debut of Stefen Fangmeier, a special-effects wizard of renown, and looks it—i.e. magically and sumptuously detailed."[12]

Readers who vividly imagine a novel's characters expect the actors who portray them in movie adaptations to live up to their imaginations. The search for *Eragon*'s lead was compared to another enormously popular fantasy novel that became a blockbuster movie: "The filmmakers conducted a worldwide casting search, which rivaled the hunt for a cinematic 'Harry Potter' and included hundreds of auditions and dozens of screen tests,"[13] explained an *Eragon* press release.

The filmmakers believed they found their lead in young actor Ed Speleers. "Ed came in [to the casting session], and we just looked at each other and said, 'That's Eragon, that's the guy from the book,"[14] remembered Fangmeier. Like Eragon, Speleers was a novice in a complicated world; prior to winning the role of Eragon, the young actor's experience was limited to school plays.

"During production in Slovakia, we were lifted by helicopter to the top of a large mountain surrounded by incredible scenery," Speleers recalled. "I stood at the edge of this mountain, thinking, 'What's going on here? I'm supposed to be at school taking my exams.' "[15]

Just as Eragon was mentored by Brom, Speleers was mentored by Jeremy Irons, an Oscar-winning actor who played Brom. "Jeremy always provided words of advice, and always nurtured me," Speleers recalled. "He was doing so out of the kindness of his heart, but at the same time so much of Brom was in Jeremy."[16]

In a review, a reviewer for the *Boston Globe* critiqued the onscreen chemistry between the film's two leads: "Speleers makes complementarily big faces; his hair, meanwhile, appears to have been colored and styled at Ye Olde Salon. . . . Played by Jeremy Irons in fits of fatigue and glee, Brom remembers life before Galbatorix's tyranny. 'There was a time when our land flourished without cruelty or fear,' he announces."[17] The critic then went on to deride the film as a whole:

> Director Stefen Fangmeier is an experienced visual-effects supervisor making his debut behind the camera, and it says a lot that the studio turned the book over to a technician and not

a visionary. *Eragon* is a handful of scenes flung at the screen. There's no rhythm or emotion holding the movie together. . . . The mess that's been made with all this money is maddening. This isn't economical moviemaking. It's a deluxe trailer for *Eragon 2*.[18]

The film Web site Rotten Tomatoes offered an opinion as to why the film version of *Eragon* was ranked among the worst of the year:

Written by a teenager (and it shows), *Eragon* presents nothing new to the "hero's journey" story archetype. In movie terms, this movie looks and sounds like *Lord of the Rings* and plays out like a bad *Star Wars* rip-off. The movie spins the tale of a peasant boy who is suddenly entrusted with a dragon and must, with the help of a mentor, train, grow strong, and defeat an evil emperor. The way the critics picture it, the makers of *Eragon* should soon be expecting an annoyed phone call from George Lucas.[19]

Audiences seemed to agree and vented their frustrations online. One such example is Jason King, a fan of the novel, who wrote on the Web site Immortal Works:

For the first twenty minutes I really tried to like this movie, but alas, I felt my heart sink as I saw Saphira instantaneously transform from a baby into a full grown dragon and then land in front of Eragon and announce, "I am your dragon, Saphira. The time for the Riders has come again." It was only downhill from there with cheesy lines, horrible acting, Saturday morning cartoon–like pacing, and drastic changes from the book that really betrayed its spirit and flavor.[20]

On December 15, 2006, *Eragon* opened on over 3,000 screens in the United States (and thousands more across the globe). While it grossed more than $20 million during its opening weekend and was number two at the box office after the Will Smith film *The Pursuit of Happyness*, it dropped a calamitous 70 percent the next weekend. By the time its theatrical run ended, it had grossed approximately $250 million. While that kind of box office is a blessing for most movies, *Eragon*'s enormous marketing and production costs meant it was barely profitable. Compared to the successful movies it tried to emulate, including *The Lord of the Rings*, *Stars Wars*, and the Harry Potter series, the movie was considered a failure. With that in mind, executives at 20th Century Fox put plans for a sequel on hold.

Christopher Paolini remained upbeat about the experience. He told reporter Claire Sutherland:

> I'm happy that a film was made at all. It certainly introduced many new readers to the series which I'm very pleased with, but ultimately the film represents the filmmaker's vision of the story and the books represent my vision of the story and people can seek out each of them on their own terms and enjoy each of them for what they are and decide which they like best.[21]

Pushed by the reporter, Paolini conceded, "Well I think they tried to do the best they could under the circumstances but the way I thought the story should be is the way it's presented in the books."[22] By early 2007, any lingering feelings about the success or failure of the movie were supplanted by a greater challenge. It looked unlikely that his third novel would be done either on time or under 1,000 pages.

In September 2008, Christopher Paolini poses with his book Brisingr. *First day sales in North America topped half a million for* Brisingr, *the third of four planned novels his million-selling Inheritance fantasy cycle.*

9

Four-part Trilogy

IT WAS JUST after midnight on September 20, 2008. Outside bookstores across the country patrons lined up, waiting for their favorite author's next work. They were not anticipating the latest book from J.K. Rowling or Stephenie Meyer. They were waiting for *Brisingr*, the third novel in Christopher Paolini's Inheritance trilogy.

Like the novels of both Rowling and Meyer, Paolini's novel "had a simultaneous worldwide release, with shops strictly forbidden from opening boxes before midnight New York time," one British newspaper reported. "Shops around the world held *Brisingr* launch parties, with U.S. events ticketed to prevent a repeat of the overwhelming number of fans who came for the release of the second book, *Eldest*."[1]

In addition to being among the first to own a copy, fans at some bookstores enjoyed parties and trivia games that began the night before. "We're thrilled to celebrate the release of *Brisingr*—a title that Christopher Paolini fans have been eagerly awaiting for months—by hosting release parties in our stores nationwide," Diane Mangan, a Borders Group merchandising director, offered. "These in-store celebrations will provide customers the opportunity to share their passion for Eragon and his adventures in a fun atmosphere filled with memorable activities."[2]

The publicity and anticipation was matched by the book's success. *Maclean's*, a Canadian news magazine, reported:

> The book sold 550,000 copies in North America in its first day, while in Britain they flew out the door at the rate of 80 a minute, not the rate of a J.K. Rowling Harry Potter release, but phenomenal nonetheless. While Paolini is now a multimillionaire, he still lives at home with his parents in Montana and doesn't have a car.[3]

The success was an amazing achievement for a writer who, less than a decade before, had conceived the trilogy

Did you know...

***Brisingr*, the title of Christopher Paolini's third book in the Inheritance Cycle, is from "The Ancient Language," a language that the author created with inspiration from the Nordic tongue. "Brisingr" means "fire."**

while in his middle teens. The first two books sold nearly 16 million copies. If there was anything that did not match the wildest dreams he once held, it was that *Brisingr* would not be the last book in the series.

"I like big books but both as an author and a reader I draw the line at 1,000 pages, so it had to be split into two," he admitted to the *Courier-Mail*. Still, his publisher did not balk at producing two books instead of one, for there was a strong possibility of sales figures being doubled. "I don't think they were disappointed, let's put it that way."[4]

Like the previous sequel, critics were divided over the book's merits. *Booklist* reviewer Daniel Kraus offered:

> In most respects, this third chapter in Paolini's Inheritance Cycle feels like the calm before the storm; the majority of the more than 700 pages are dominated by storytelling, plotting, and preparations for battle. If there is a complaint from readers, it will be that Paolini revels too much in long conversations between his characters while action takes a backseat, but fans of the genre will bask in his generosity: the arcana of dwarf election rules, the manhood customs of the Kull, and the finer points on forging a Dragon Rider's sword are all part of what makes the world of Alagaësia so encompassing.[5]

The third novel's story follows Eragon helping his cousin Roran to rescue his true love Katrina from the deadly Ra'zac, while the Varden prepares to battle King Galbatorix. "Most of the combat—and it's brutal, gory stuff—belongs to Roran as he becomes a legendary warrior; Eragon's struggles are more cerebral and involve magic, a difficult thing to dramatize but something Paolini pulls off admirably," Kraus continued. "In fact, clarity is the author's best asset: few could make such a Tolkienesque universe so manageable. Anyone who couldn't wait for this volume will be just as excited when the upcoming fourth and final chapter appears."[6]

While Kraus found much to enjoy, *School Library Journal* reviewer Edith Ching felt:

> [*Brisingr*] "spends a great deal of time giving background information about earlier connections and obligations . . . Both heroes [Eragon and Roran] grow in their understanding of themselves and others as they assume additional leadership roles . . . [while] Saphira's point of view adds additional dimension to the tale. There is a lot of talking in this book, which slows down the pace.[7]

LIFE BEYOND A FOURTH BOOK

Paolini had been a best-selling author for only a few weeks when he began to imagine what his life would be like once he concluded Eragon's story. "I might go to college," he told a reporter in 2003. "Or I might take a vacation and have a nervous breakdown. I have a lot of reading to do, *Ulysses*, Dostoyevsky, the rest of Tolstoy."[8]

Now in his twenties, Christopher Paolini has reached an age when many adults are beginning their careers and starting families. Yet, despite all of his success as a fantasy author, Paolini has remained the same since reaching adulthood. In 2005, a reporter noted:

> [Paolini] has no plans to go to college at this point or even to start going on dates. He's going to keep doing what he has been doing for the past six years: writing from breakfast till an hour before dinner, seven days a week, every week of the year except for Christmas, until the adventure is over for him as much as for Eragon.[9]

When will that be? "As soon as I possibly can," he told Claire Sutherland in the fall of 2008. "I'm afraid I can't be any more definite than that. I have started the fourth book and I will be returning to it as soon as I get back from the book tour."[10]

There are, he admits, quite a few loose ends in Eragon's tale—unresolved conflicts that need resolving. And in a series that boasts hundreds of characters and a unique language, that will take some doing. "Sometimes I'll call up the head of the largest fan site here in the U.S. and ask him if I forgot something from one of the earlier books," he confesses. "He's got a great mind for this stuff and he's a really nice guy and a big fan, obviously, and I always enjoy talking with him."[11]

He knows he has to finish the series and has no plans to add to it following the publication of the fourth book. According to Paolini, the fourth book will be the final one in the Inheritance Cycle because, as he admitted in 2005, "That's actually one of the things that truly bugs me as a reader, the fact that so many series drag on and on without achieving a true end. You can't have a good story without a good end."[12]

While the story of Eragon may reach its conclusion, the story of Christopher Paolini—once a homeschooled teen who has now written a best-selling fantasy series—is far from over. For while this story has consumed nearly half his life, there are, he admits, more stories left to tell.

CHRONOLOGY

1983 Christopher Paolini is born on November 17 in California.

1987–1991 Paolini's parents, Kenneth and Talita, decide to leave the Church Universal and Triumphant (CUT). The family moves to Alaska.

1988 Talita decides to educate their children, Christopher and Angela, at home using the Montessori Method.

1991 The Paolini family settles in Montana.

1998 After graduating from the American School of Correspondence in Chicago, Illinois, Christopher Paolini begins outlining a trilogy, then begins writing the first book in the series, *Eragon.*

1999 With the first draft of *Eragon* completed, he begins rewriting it on his own.

2000 The second draft of *Eragon* dismays its author and he asks his parents for help with the revisions. Kenneth Paolini believes with work it could be successfully self-published.

2001 Paolini is accepted at Reed University in Portland, Oregon. He delays admission as *Eragon* is finally ready for publication. Kenneth Paolini formats it with Adobe PageMaker and the family discusses how to best sell the book.

2002 Paolini sells his book in stores and at schools where he gives the presentation "Why Read? Why Write?" more than 150 times. On a summer vacation, best-selling novelist Carl Hiaasen buys *Eragon* for his stepson. Hiaasen then reads it, likes it, and sends it to his publisher. Knopf Publishing buys the rights to *Eragon* and the rest of the trilogy for six figures.

2003 *Eragon* is published; it is an immediate bestseller.

2004 The film studio 20th Century Fox buys the film rights to *Eragon*. Paolini begins work on his second novel, *Eldest*.

2005 *Eldest* is published; it is also a bestseller.

2006 The movie *Eragon* is released.

2008 *Brisingr*, the third book in the series, is released. By now Paolini's novels have sold nearly 20 million copies worldwide.

NOTES

Chapter 1

1 "Contemporary Authors Online." Gale, 2009. Reproduced in *Biography Resource Center*. Farmington Hills, Mich.: Gale, 2009.

2 Ibid.

3 "Carl Hiaasen on Chris Paolini Self-Published *Eragon*." http://www.youtube.com/watch?v=fZ734utZM4U.

4 Ibid.

5 Michael Shelden, "Meet the 21st-Century Tolkien," (London) *Telegraph*, December 22, 2003. http://www.telegraph.co.uk/culture/donotmigrate/3608974/Meet-the-21st-century-Tolkien.html.

6 Carol Memmott, "Wizard of Words Writes Away," *USA Today*, August 30, 2005. http://www.usatoday.com/life/books/news/2005-08-30-paolini_x.htm.

7 "Christopher Paolini," Author Interview at Teenreads.com, September 2003. http://www.teenreads.com/authors/au-paolini-christopher.asp.

Chapter 2

1 "Church Universal and Triumphant," AllAboutCults.org. http://www.allaboutcults.org/church-universal-and-triumphant.htm.

2 Elizabeth Clare Prophet, *Religious Leaders of America*, 2nd ed. Gale, 1999. Reproduced in *Biography Resource Center*. Farmington Hills, Mich.: Gale, 2009.

3 Jim Jones, *World of Criminal Justice*, 2 vols. Gale, 2002. Reproduced in *Biography Resource Center*. Farmington Hills, Mich.: Gale, 2009.

4 Ibid.

5 Dinitia Smith, "Finding a Middle Earth in Montana; A Teenager's Fantasy Set in a Magical Land Is a Best Seller," *New York Times*, October 7, 2003, p. E1.

6 Ibid.

7 Scott McMillion, "CUT Undergoes Change of Perception," *Bozeman Daily Chronicle*, March 13, 2005.

8 Ibid.

9 Smith, "Finding a Middle Earth in Montana."

10 "Contemporary Authors Online," Gale, 2009. Reproduced in *Biography Resource Center*. Farmington Hills, Mich.: Gale, 2009.

11 Christopher Paolini, "Dragon Tales: An Essay by Christopher Paolini on Becoming a Writer," BookBrowse, March 23, 2009. http://www.bookbrowse.com/author_interviews/full/index.cfm?author_number=934.

12 Christopher Paolini, "Dragon Tales," Author Talk: September

2003 at Teenreads.com. http://www.teenreads.com/authors/au-paolini-christopher.asp.

13 Claire Sutherland, "Homeschool Author Christopher Paolini Hits Big Time," (London) *Courier-Mail*, October 4, 2008. http://www.news.comau/couriermail/story/0,23739,24435244-5003424,00.html.

14 Denise Oliveri, "How to Homeschool in Montana," eHow, September 26, 2009. http://www.ehow.com_2227008_home school-in-Montana.html.

15 Smith, "Finding a Middle Earth in Montana."

16 Ibid.

17 Paolini, "Dragon Tales," BookBrowse.

18 Natalie Canavor, "More School Bells Ring at Home," *New York Times*, August 21, 2005, p. LI1.

19 Smith, "Finding a Middle Earth in Montana."

20 "Teenage Master of Monsters," (London) *Telegraph*, October 27, 2003.

21 "Christopher Paolini," Author Interview at Teenreads.com.

22 Elizabeth Winchester, "Christopher Paolini, Author: TFK Talks to This Teenage Author About his Best-selling First Book *Eragon*," *Time For Kids*, October 6, 2003. http://www.timeforkids.com/TFK/class/area/newsarticleprintout/0,17447,516153,00.html.

23 Stephen King, *On Writing: A Memoir of the Craft*, New York: Pocket Books, 2000, p. 147.

24 Seamus Heaney, *Beowulf: An Illustrated Edition.* New York: W.W. Norton, 2000, p. vii.

25 Harold Bloom, "Introduction," *Modern Critical Views: J.R.R. Tolkien*, Philadelphia: Chelsea House, 2000. p. 1.

26 Ibid., "Tolkien and Frodo Baggins," p. 35.

27 Christopher Paolini, "Dragon Tales," Author Talk.

28 Ibid.

Chapter 3

1 Sutherland, "Homeschool Author Christopher Paolini Hits Big Time."

2 Ursula K. Le Guin, "Why Are Americans Afraid of Dragons?" *The Language of the Night.* New York: HarperCollins, 1979, rev. 1988. p. 40.

3 Maria Scherrer, "Interview with Christopher Paolini," Literaturschock, September 12, 2004. http://www.literaturschock.de/autorengefluester/000081.

4 Sutherland, "Homeschool Author Christopher Paolini Hits Big Time."

5 Memmott, "Wizard of Words Writes Away."

6 Natalie Goldberg, *Writing Down the Bones: Freeing the Writer Within*. Boston: Shambhala, 1986, p. 48.

7 "Richard Wagner," *Encyclopedia of World Biography*, 2nd ed. 17 Vols. Gale, 1998. Reproduced in *Biography Resource Center.* Farmington Hills, Mich.: Gale, 2009.

8 Ibid.

9 David Weich, "Philip Pullman, Tamora Pierce, and Christopher Paolini Talk Fantasy Fiction," Powells.com, July 31, 2003. http://www.powells.com/authors/paolini.html.

10 Barbara Frank, "Christopher Paolini and *Eragon*: A Home-school Success Story." http://homeschooling.gomilpitas.com/articles/052504.htm.

11 Christopher Paolini, "How I Write," *The Writer*, January 30, 2004. http://www.writermag.com/wrt/default.aspx?c=a&id=1415.

12 Paolini, "Dragon Tales," Author Talk.

13 King, *On Writing*, pp.158–159.

14 Orson Scott Card, "The Hero and the Common Man," *Characters and Viewpoint*, Cincinnati: Writer's Digest Books, 1988, p. 96.

15 Paolini, "How I Write."

16 King, *On Writing*, p.156.

17 "Christopher Paolini Biography," BookBrowse. http://www.bookbrowse.com/biographies/index.cfm?author_number=934.

18 Paolini, "Dragon Tales," Author Talk.

19 Ibid.

20 "Christopher Paolini Biography," BookBrowse.

21 Weich, "Philip Pullman, Tamora Pierce, and Christopher Paolini Talk Fantasy Fiction."

22 Le Guin, "Why Are Americans Afraid of Dragons?"

23 "C.G. Jung," *Scientists: Their Lives and Works*, Vols. 1–7. Online Edition. U*X*L, 2006. Reproduced in *Biography Resource Center*. Farmington Hills, Mich.: Gale, 2009.

24 Liz Rosenberg, "The Egg and Him," *New York Times*, November 16, 2003, p. B34.

25 Joseph Campbell, "About the Author," *The Hero With a Thousand Faces*, Novato, Calif.: New World Library, 1949, rev. 2008, p. 415.

26 Ibid., p. 23.

27 Memmott, "Wizard of Words Writes Away."

28 Paolini, "Dragon Tales," Author Talk.

29 Ibid.

Chapter 4

1 Christopher Paolini, *Eragon*, New York: Alfred A. Knopf, 2002, p. 64.

2 Ibid., p. 430.

3 Paolini, "Dragon Tales," Author Talk.

4 King, *On Writing*, pp. 210–211.

5 Shelden, "Meet the 21st-Century Tolkien."

6 Weich, "Philip Pullman, Tamora Pierce, and Christopher Paolini Talk Fantasy Fiction."

7 Anne Lamott, *Bird by Bird: Some Instructions on Writing and Life*, New York: Random House, 1994, pp. 21–22.

8 Paolini, "Dragon Tales: An Essay by Christopher Paolini on Becoming a Writer."

9 Paolini, "Dragon Tales," Author Talk.

10 Ibid.

11 Shelden, "Meet the 21st-Century Tolkien."

12 "Christopher Paolini," Interview at Teenreads.com.

13 Nancy Varian Berberick, "Certain of What We Do Not See," *How to Write Tales of Horror, Fantasy & Science Fiction*, J.N. Williamson, ed. Cincinnati: Writer's Digest Books, 1987, p. 3.

14 Ibid.

15 Darrell Schweitzer, "Sword and Sorcery, Dragon and Princess," *How to Write Tales of Horror, Fantasy and Science Fiction*, J.N. Williamson, ed. Cincinnati: Writer's Digest Books, 1987, p.78.

16 "Christopher Paolini," Interview at Teenreads.com.

17 Paolini, "How I Write."

18 Le Guin, *The Language of the Night*, New York: HarperCollins, 1979, rev. 1988, p. 85.

19 Ibid., p. 91.

20 "Teenage Master of Monsters."

21 Christopher Paolini, "On Writing," Author Talk: September 2003. http://www.teenreads.com/authors/au-paolini-christopher.asp.

Chapter 5

1 Paolini, "On Writing."

2 Winchester, "Christopher Paolini, Author."

3 Elham Khatami, "More Authors Turn to Web and Print-on-Demand Publishing," CNN.com, http://www.cnn.com/2009/TECH/04/06/print.on.demand.publishing/index.html.

4 Ibid.

5 Yvonne Zipp, "Teen Author Wins Readers Book by Book," *Christian Science Monitor*, August 7, 2003, p. 20.

6 Paolini, "Dragon Tales," Author Talk.

7 Weich, "Philip Pullman, Tamora Pierce, and Christopher Paolini Talk Fantasy Fiction."

8 Christopher Paolini, "Dragon Tales," Author Talk.

9 Reed College, "About Reed: Mission and History," http://www.reed.edu/about_reed/history.html.

10 Ibid.

11 Paolini, "Dragon Tales: An Essay by Christopher Paolini on Becoming a Writer."

12 Paolini, "Dragon Tales," Author Talk.

13 Shelden, "Meet the 21st-Century Tolkien."

14 Sutherland, "Homeschool Author Christopher Paolini Hits Big Time."

15 Ibid.

16 Scherrer, "Interview with Christopher Paolini."

17 "Teenage Master of Monsters."

18 Lev Grossman, "Books: Christopher Paolini: The Real-Life Boy Wizard," *Time*, August 21, 2005. http://www.time.com/time/printout/0,8816,1096484,00.html.

19 Shelden, "Meet the 21st-Century Tolkien."

20 Smith, "Finding a Middle Earth in Montana."

21 Shelden, "Meet the 21st-Century Tolkien."

22 Sutherland, "Homeschool Author Christopher Paolini Hits Big Time."

23 Mike Williams, "Hiaasen Tackles 'Rodent' That Ate Florida," *Atlanta Journal-Constitution*, June 14, 1998, p. L11.

24 Shelden, "Meet the 21st-Century Tolkien."

25 Ibid.

Chapter 6

1 Smith, "Finding a Middle Earth in Montana."

2 Christopher Paolini, *Eldest*, New York: Alfred A. Knopf, 2005, p. 678.

3 Sutherland, "Homeschool Author Christopher Paolini Hits Big Time."

4 Memmott, "Wizard of Words Writes Away."

5 Jay MacDonald, "Fantastic Voyage: Dragon Saga Launches Paolini into Publishing Stratosphere," *First Person BookPage*, September 2005. http://www.bookpage.com/0509bp/christopher_paolini.html.

6 Memmott, "Wizard of Words Writes Away."

7 Paolini, "How I Write."

8 Memmott, "Wizard of Words Writes Away."

9 MacDonald, "Fantastic Voyage: Dragon Saga Launches Paolini into Publishing Stratosphere."

10 Sutherland, "Homeschool Author Christopher Paolini Hits Big Time."

11 Paolini, "On Writing."

12 Rosenberg, "The Egg and Him."

13 Ibid.

14 Paolini, "How I Write."

15 Susan L. Rogers, "Review of *Eragon*," *School Library Journal*, September 1, 2003, p. 218.

16 Paolini, "On Writing."

Chapter 7

1 Shelden, "Meet the 21st-Century Tolkien."

2 Ibid.

3 Paolini, "How I Write."

4 MacDonald, "Fantastic Voyage: Dragon Saga Launches Paolini into Publishing Stratosphere."

5 Weich, "Philip Pullman, Tamora Pierce, and Christopher Paolini Talk Fantasy Fiction."

6 Louis Giannetti, *Understanding Movies*, Fifth Ed., Englewood Cliffs, N.J.: Prentice Hall, 1990, pp. 441–442.

7 Grossman, "Books: Christopher Paolini: The Real-Life Boy Wizard."

8 Weich, "Philip Pullman, Tamora Pierce, and Christopher Paolini Talk Fantasy Fiction."

9 Jennifer Reese, "Book Review: *Eragon*," *Entertainment Weekly*, August 24, 2005. http://www.ew.com/ew/article/0,,1095866,00.html.

10 Ibid.

11 "*Eldest* Review," *Publishers Weekly*, July 25, 2005, v. 252i, p. 78.

12 Paolini, *Eldest*, p. 542.

13 Ibid., pp. 542–543.

14 Sutherland, "Homeschool Author Christopher Paolini Hits Big Time."

15 Ibid.

16 Weich, "Philip Pullman, Tamora Pierce, and Christopher Paolini Talk Fantasy Fiction."

17 "Random House Press Release–August 30, 2005." http://www.

randomhouse.biz/media/pdfs/EldestPressRel.pdf.

18 Paolini, *Eldest*, p. 677.

Chapter 8

1 Goldberg, *Writing Down the Bones*, p. 79.

2 "Teenage Master of Monsters."

3 Eddie Dorman Kay, *Box Office Champs: The Most Popular Movies of the Last Fifty Years*. New York: Random House, 1990, p. 146.

4 "Interview with Christopher Paolini at Premiere of *Eragon*, December 15, 2006," IGN Entertainment—Fox Entertainment Media. http://movies.ign.com/dor/objects/40599/eragon/videos/eragon_red_chirstopher.html.

5 "Dragons of the Silver and Small Screen," Here Be Dragons! http://www.draconian.com/movie/movie.php.

6 "20th Century Fox Press Release for *Eragon* the Motion Picture." http://www.shurtugal.com/content/mandm/eragon/prodnotes.pdf.

7 Ibid.

8 Ibid.

9 Justin Chang, "*Eragon*," *Variety*, December 15, 2006. http://www.variety.com/review/VE1117932309.html?categoryid=31&cs=1.

10 "20th Century Fox Press Release for *Eragon* the Motion Picture."

11 Chang, "*Eragon*."

12 Joe Morgenstern "Cute Dragon Fires Up *Eragon*," *Wall Street Journal*, December 15, 2006. http://online.wsj.com/article/SB116614157691750720.html.4

13 "20th Century Fox Press Release for *Eragon* the Motion Picture."

14 Ibid.

15 Ibid.

16 Ibid.

17 Wesley Morris, "Even Dragons Can't Get *Eragon* Off the Ground," *Boston Globe*, December 15, 2006. http://www.boston.com/movies/display?display=movie&id=7982.

18 Ibid.

19 "*Eragon* (2006)," Reviewed at RottenTomatoes.com. http://au.rottentomatoes.com/m/eragon/.

20 Jason King, "*Eragon*: A Story Lost in Translation," Immortal Works. http://www.immortalworks.net/page14/page15/page15.php.

21 Sutherland, "Homeschool Author Christopher Paolini Hits Big Time."

22 Ibid.

Chapter 9

1 Sutherland, "Homeschool Author Christopher Paolini Hits Big Time."

2 "Borders and Waldenbooks Stores to Celebrate the Release of Christopher Paolini's *Brisingr* with Parties Nationwide Sept. 19 and 20," PR Newswire, September 5, 2008. http://www.encyclopedia.com/doc/1G1-185921186.html.

3 "Christopher Paolini: the Next J.K. Rowling," *Maclean's*, October 13, 2008, v. 121, p. 119.

4 Sutherland, "Homeschool Author Christopher Paolini Hits Big Time."

5 Daniel Kraus, "*Brisingr*," *Booklist*, November 1, 2008, v. 105 i5, p. 34.

6 Ibid.

7 Edith Ching, "*Brisingr*: Inheritance, Book 3," *School Library Journal*, February 2009, v. 55 i2, pp. 55–56.

8 Smith, "Finding a Middle Earth in Montana."

9 Grossman, "Books: Christopher Paolini: The Real-Life Boy Wizard."

10 Sutherland, "Homeschool Author Christopher Paolini Hits Big Time."

11 Ibid.

12 MacDonald, "Fantastic Voyage: Dragon Saga Launches Paolini Publishing Stratosphere."

WORKS BY CHRISTOPHER PAOLINI

2003 *Eragon*

2005 *Eldest*

2008 *Brisingr*

2009 *Eragon's Guide to Alagaësia*

POPULAR BOOKS

ERAGON

After an orphaned farm boy named Eragon discovers a blue dragon egg, he learns he is destined to become a Dragon Rider. Leaving his home to escape the Empire, he trains in magic and fighting with Brom, a former rider.

ELDEST

While Eragon continues his training in magic and sword craft in the secretive elf home of Ellesméra, his cousin Roran leads a band of villagers fleeing from the Empire.

BRISINGR

As Eragon continues his training in magic, he prepares to assist the Varden in their war with the Empire as his cousin Roran develops into a skilled warrior.

POPULAR CHARACTERS

BROM

Although initially viewed as only an amusing storyteller, Brom is actually a former Dragon Rider. He begins Eragon's training in magic and fighting.

ERAGON

The title character of the first book in the Inheritance Cycle, the 15-year-old Eragon reflects some of the emotions of the author, who was also 15 when he began writing the novel.

KING GALBATORIX

Once a Dragon Rider, Galbatorix has held the empire in his violent grip for over a century.

NASUADA

The leader of the Varden, Nasuada tries to ally the dwarves and humans against the Empire.

OROMIS

An ancient elf who continues Eragon's training.

RORAN

Although he resents the danger his cousin Eragon has brought to his village, Roran nevertheless fights beside him against the Empire.

SAPHIRA

Rescued as an egg, the dragon grows to adulthood under Eragon's devoted care.

MAJOR AWARDS

2004 *Eragon* wins Booklist's Top Ten Books for Youth in the SF/Fantasy category.

2006 *Eragon* wins the Rebecca Caudill Young Readers' Book Award; *Eldest* earns the Quill Award in the Young Adult/Teen category.

BIBLIOGRAPHY

Books

Bloom, Harold. *Modern Critical Views: J.R.R. Tolkien*. Philadelphia: Chelsea House, 2000.

Campbell, Joseph. *The Hero With a Thousand Faces*. Novato, Calif.: New World Library, 1949, rev. 2008.

Card, Orson Scott. *Characters and Viewpoint*. Cincinnati: Writer's Digest Books, 1988.

Giannetti, Louis. *Understanding Movies*, Fifth Ed. Englewood Cliffs, N.J.: Prentice Hall, 1990.

Gunn, James. *The Science of Science-Fiction Writing.* Lanham, Md.: The Scarecrow Press, 2000.

Heaney, Seamus. *Beowulf: An Illustrated Edition.* New York: W.W. Norton, 2000.

Kay, Eddie Dorman. *Box Office Champs: The Most Popular Movies of the Last Fifty Years*. New York: Random House, 1990.

King, Stephen. *On Writing: A Memoir of the Craft.* New York: Pocket Books, 2000.

Lamott, Anne. *Bird by Bird: Some Instructions on Writing and Life.* New York: Random House, 1994.

Le Guin, Ursula K. *The Language of the Night*. New York: HarperCollins, 1979, rev. 1988.

Strunk Jr., William, and White, E.B. *The Elements of Style: Everything You Need to Know to Write*, Fourth Ed. New York: Longman, 2009.

Williamson, J.N., ed. *How to Write Tales of Horror, Fantasy & Science Fiction*. Cincinnati: Writer's Digest Books, 1987.

Periodicals

Canavor, Natalie. "More School Bells Ring at Home." *New York Times*. August 21, 2005: p. LI1.

"C.G. Jung." *Scientists: Their Lives and Works*, Vols. 1–7. Online Edition. U*X*L, 2006. Reproduced in *Biography Resource Center*. Farmington Hills, Mich.: Gale, 2009.

Chang, Justin. "*Eragon*." *Variety*. December 15, 2006. Available online. URL: http://www.variety.com/review/VE1117932309.html?categoryid=31&cs=1.

Ching, Edith. "*Brisingr*: Inheritance, Book 3." *School Library Journal*. February 2009 v. 55 i2: pp. 55–56.

"Christopher Paolini: the Next J.K. Rowling." *Maclean's*, October 13, 2008 v. 121: p. 119.

"*Eldest* Review." *Publishers Weekly*. July 25, 2005 v. 252i: p. 78.

Grossman, Lev. "Books: Christopher Paolini: The Real-Life Boy Wizard." *Time*. August 21, 2005. Available online. URL: http://www.time.com/time/printout/0,8816,1096484,00.html.

Jones, Jim. *World of Criminal Justice*, 2 vols. Gale, 2002. Reproduced in *Biography Resource Center*. Farmington Hills, Mich.: Gale, 2009.

Kraus, Daniel. "*Brisingr*." *Booklist*. November 1, 2008 v. 105 i5: p. 34.

MacDonald, Jay. "Fantastic Voyage: Dragon Saga Launches Paolini into Publishing Stratosphere." *First Person BookPage*. September 2005. Available online. URL: http://www.bookpage.com/0509bp/christopher_paolini.html.

McMillion, Scott. "CUT Undergoes Change of Perception." *Bozeman Daily Chronicle*. March 13, 2005.

Memmott, Carol. "Wizard of Words Writes Away." *USA Today*. August 30, 2005. Available online. URL: http://www.usatoday.com/life/books/news/2005-08-30-paolini_x.htm.

Morgenstern, Joe. "Cute Dragon Fires Up *Eragon*." *Wall Street Journal*. December 15, 2006. Available online. URL: http://online.wsj.com/article/SB116614157691750720.html.

Morris, Wesley. "Even Dragons Can't Get *Eragon* Off the Ground." *Boston Globe*. December 15, 2006. Available online. URL: http://www.boston.com/movies/display?display=movie&id=7982.

Paolini, Christopher. "How I Write." *The Writer*. January 30, 2004. Available online. URL: http://www.writermag.com/wrt/default.aspx?c=a&id=1415.

Prophet, Elizabeth Clare. *Religious Leaders of America*, 2nd ed. Gale, 1999. Reproduced in *Biography Resource Center*. Farmington Hills, Mich.: Gale, 2009.

Reese, Jennifer. "Book Review: *Eragon*." *Entertainment Weekly*. August 24, 2005 i836: p. 64.

"Richard Wagner." *Encyclopedia of World Biography*, 2nd ed. 17 Vols. Gale, 1998. Reproduced in *Biography Resource Center*. Farmington Hills, Mich.: Gale, 2009.

Rogers, Susan L. "Review of *Eragon*." *School Library Journal*. September 1, 2003: p. 218.

Rosenberg, Liz. "The Egg and Him." *New York Times*. November 16, 2003: p. B34.

Shelden, Michael. "Meet the 21st-Century Tolkien." (London) *Telegraph*. December 22, 2003. Available online. URL: http://www.telegraph.co.uk/culture/donotmigrate/3608974/Meet-the-21st-century-Tolkien.html.

Smith, Dinitia. "Finding a Middle Earth in Montana; A Teenager's Fantasy Set in a Magical Land Is a Best Seller." *New York Times*. October 7, 2003: p. E1.

Sutherland, Claire. "Homeschool Author Christopher Paolini Hits Big Time." (London) *Courier-Mail*. October 3, 2008. Available online. URL: http://www.news.comau/couriermail/story/0,23739,24435244-5003424,00.html.

"Teenage Master of Monsters." (London) *Telegraph*. October 27, 2003.

Williams, Mike. "Hiaasen Tackles 'Rodent' That Ate Florida." *Atlanta Journal-Constitution*. June 14, 1998: p. L11.

Winchester, Elizabeth. "Christopher Paolini, Author: TFK Talks to This Teenage Author About his Best-selling First Book *Eragon*." *Time For Kids*. October 6, 2003. Available online. URL: http://www.timeforkids.com/TFK/class/area/newsarticleprintout/0,17447,516153,00.html.

Zipp, Yvonne. "Teen Author Wins Readers Book by Book." *Christian Science Monitor*. August 7, 2003: p. 20.

Web Sites

"20th Century Fox Press Release for *Eragon* the Motion Picture." Available online. URL: http://www.shurtugal.com/content/mandm/eragon/prodnotes.pdf.

American School. Available online. URL: http://www.americanschoolofcorr.com/grads.asp.

"Borders and Waldenbooks Stores to Celebrate the Release of Christopher Paolini's *Brisingr* with Parties Nationwide Sept. 19 and 20." PR Newswire, September 5, 2008. Available online. URL: http://www.encyclopedia.com/doc/1G1-185921186.html.

"Carl Hiaasen on Chris Paolini Self-Published *Eragon*." Available online. URL: http://www.youtube.com/watch?v=fZ734utZM4U.

"Christopher Paolini." Author Interview at Teenreads.com. September 2003. Available online. URL: http://www.teenreads.com/authors/au-paolini-christopher.asp.

"Christopher Paolini Biography." BookBrowse. Available online. URL: http://www.bookbrowse.com/biographies/index.cfm?author_number=934.

"Church Universal and Triumphant." AllAboutCults.org. Available online. URL: http://www.allaboutcults.org/church-universal-and-triumphant.htm.

"Dragons of the Silver and Small Screen." Here Be Dragons! Available online. URL: http://www.draconian.com/movie/movie.php.

"*Eragon* (2006)." Reviewed at RottenTomatoes.com. Available online. URL: http://au.rottentomatoes.com/m/eragon/.

Frank, Barbara. "Christopher Paolini and *Eragon*: A Homeschool Success Story." Available online. URL: http://homeschooling.gomilpitas.com/articles/052504.htm.

"Interview with Christopher Paolini at Premiere of *Eragon*, December 15, 2006." IGN Entertainment—Fox Entertainment Media. Available online. URL: http://movies.ign.com/dor/objects/40599/eragon/videos/eragon_red_chirstopher.html.

Khatami, Elham. "More Authors Turn to Web and Print-on-Demand Publishing." CNN.com. Available online. URL: http://www.cnn.com/2009/TECH/04/06/print.on.demand.publishing/index.html.

King, Jason. "*Eragon*: A Story Lost in Translation." Immortal Works. Available online. URL: http://www.immortalworks.net/page14/page15/page15.php.

Oliveri, Denise. "How to Homeschool in Montana." eHow. September 26, 2009. Available online. URL: http://www.ehow.com/how_2227008_homeschool-in-montana.html.

Paolini, Christopher. "Dragon Tales: An Essay by Christopher Paolini on Becoming a Writer." BookBrowse. March 23, 2009. Available online. URL: http://www.bookbrowse.com/author_interviews/full/index.cfm?author_number=934.

———. "Dragon Tales," Author Talk: September 2003 at Teenreads.com. Available online. URL: http://www.teenreads.com/authors/au-paolini-christopher.asp.

"Random House Press Release–August 30, 2005." Available online. URL: http://www.randomhouse.biz/media/pdfs/EldestPressRel.pdf.

Reed College. "About Reed: Mission and History." Available online. URL: http://www.reed.edu/about_reed/history.html.

Scherrer, Maria. "Interview mit Christopher Paolini." Literaturschock. September 12, 2004. Available online. URL: http://www.literaturschock.de/autorengefluester/000081.

Weich, David. "Philip Pullman, Tamora Pierce, and Christopher Paolini Talk Fantasy Fiction." Powells.com. July 31, 2003. Available online. URL: http://www.powells.com/authors/paolini.html.

FURTHER READING

Books

Bradbury, Ray. *Zen in the Art of Writing: Releasing the Creative Genius in You*. Santa Barbara, Calif.: Capra Press, 1990.

Goldberg, Natalie. *Writing Down the Bones: Freeing the Writer Within*. Boston: Shambhala, 1986.

Web Sites

Eragon, Eldest, and Brisingr Official Site
http://www.alagaesia.com

Random House—Pullman, Paolini, Pierce
http://www.randomhouse.com/teens/3ps/

Shurtugal
http://www.shurtugal.com

PICTURE CREDITS

page:

10: Maury Phillips/WireImage/ Getty Images

16: Matthew Brown/AP Images

19: Greg Robinson/AP Images

23: © Dale Spartas/Corbis

34: © Lebrecht Music and Arts Photo Library/Alamy

41: © William Campbell/Corbis

45: © Bettmann/CORBIS

50: Haywood Magee/Picture Post/ Hulton Archive/Getty Images

56: © William Campbell/ Corbis

60: © dk/Alamy

72: CHIP EAST/Reuters/ Landov

78: Orlin Wagner/AP Images

82: © Photos 12/Alamy

90: 20th Century Fox/Photofest

96: Dave Hogan/Getty Images Entertainment/Getty Images

102: David Grubbs/AP Images

INDEX

Page numbers in *italics* indicate photos or illustrations.

ABOUT THE CONTRIBUTOR

Born in Boston, Massachusetts, **JOHN BANKSTON** spent his teen years in a Vermont log cabin without a television. He began writing articles while still a teenager. Since then, more than 200 of his articles have been published in magazines and newspapers across the country, including *The Tallahassee Democrat*, *The Orlando Sentinel*, and *The Tallahassean*. He is the author of more than 60 biographies for young adults, including works on scientist Stephen Hawking, anthropologist Margaret Mead, author F. Scott Fitzgerald, and actor Heath Ledger. He lives on Balboa Island in Newport Beach, California.